CW00468815

A COWBOY AND HIS MISTLETOE KISS

A Johnson Brothers Novel, Chestnut Ranch Romance, Book 2

EMMY EUGENE

Copyright © 2020 by Emmy Eugene

All rights reserved.

No part of this book may be reproduced in any form or by any electronic or
mechanical means, including information storage and retrieval systems, without
written permission from the author, except for the use of brief quotations in a
book review.

ISBN-13: 978-1659746563

CHAPTER ONE

Travis Johnson pulled at the tightness of his tie around his neck. He didn't attend church all that often, and so didn't wear a white shirt and tie much. And since it was his older brother who'd gotten married tonight, he not only wore a white shirt and tie, but a fancy suit coat to match the slick, pressed slacks he currently wore.

At least Seth had allowed cowboy hats and cowboy boots as part of the wedding-approved attire. If he hadn't, there might have been a brotherly mutiny on his hands.

As it was, Travis felt stuffed into a monkey suit, sipping punch, and wishing he could leave early.

But the dinner had just started, and then there was dancing. And cake-cutting. And then the big sparkler send-off as Seth and Jenna went blissfully on their honeymoon for the next two weeks.

Travis was already dreading trying to do the work of three men where there were only two of them at the homestead now. Seth had moved almost everything he owned into Jenna's house next door yesterday after they'd all shared Thanksgiving together at their parents' house.

Seth had still slept at the homestead, but it already felt too empty without him there. Travis got along great with Russ; that wasn't a problem. Taking on Seth's dog operation was, as it had swelled to astronomical numbers since the article in the Texas Hill Country magazine had hit virtual shelves.

Not only that, but Gertrude Wisehouse had run a piece in the town's newsletter, and it felt like a new dog got dropped off at Chestnut Ranch every single day. Seth, Travis, and Russ had talked a lot about putting a system in place for drop-offs, but nothing much had come of it yet. Seth really didn't want to turn away dogs in need, and truth be told, Travis couldn't stomach the idea of that either.

A waiter arrived at his table, and plates of food got served. He waited until everyone at the table had food, and then he picked up his knife and fork.

"At least the food is delicious," Russ said from beside him.

"Yeah." He cut into his steak, which was perfectly cooked. Rex and Griffin sat at the table with them, as did their parents and Jenna's brother, Isaac. That completed the family table, though Travis had cousins seated at a nearby table, and he knew almost everyone else in the banquet hall as well.

"The wedding was beautiful," his mother said for the third time in the twenty minutes since the ceremony had ended. She sniffed and reached for her glass of sweet tea. "It sure would be nice if some more of you boys could get married."

"Momma," Griffin said. "Talk to Russ. He's the one with the serious girlfriend."

"Uh," Russ said, his face coloring.

Travis instantly felt bad for his brother, because he knew what the others at the table didn't.

"Uh, what?" Rex asked, not about to let that slide.

Russ looked at Travis, a pleading expression on his face. "He broke up with Janelle," he said.

"No," Russ barked. "*She* broke up with *me*."

Which was worse, Travis knew. "Sorry," he said at the same time Griffin said, "What? How is that possible?"

Rex added, "You guys were like, *awesome* together."

Surprisingly, their mother didn't say anything, and Travis looked across the table to where Jenna's brother sat. He seemed enthralled by the Johnson family drama, and Travis smiled at him.

"We're not usually crazy," he said.

"Oh, I know how you guys are," Isaac said with a laugh. "And this is mild."

Travis couldn't deny it, so he just shrugged. Russ kept his head down and his hat low, blocking anyone from seeing his face. Travis knew just how he felt. Rex had been going out with women like he was trying on a new pair of boots. Griffin had been out a few times, but nothing was sticking, and he wouldn't go out with anyone Rex had already taken to dinner.

Travis had met two women at the speed dating event during Octoberfest that had caught his interest. He'd gone out with Flora Thompson three times before she'd told him there was no spark for her.

That had kept the second number he'd gotten stuffed away in his wallet. There, but not forgotten. Not used either.

Millie Hepworth was a gorgeous blonde he'd actually been out with once before. Maybe twice. Fine, at least half a dozen times. Then she'd moved for a job, and Travis had thought he'd never see her again.

But there she'd been, at the speed dating event, only a resident of Chestnut Springs for a week. He'd gotten her number, but he wasn't blind. Several other men there had liked Millie too, and Travis was nothing if not great at Internet spying.

So he'd seen Millie's pictures of her and her new boyfriend, a man named Mitchell Anders. And Mitch was a good guy. Maybe a little stuffy, in Travis's opinion, but he supposed people could classify him as standoffish.

He wasn't; he was just more reserved than some of the other Johnson brothers. He preferred to hang out at the back of the crowd and only say something if he needed to.

He hadn't called Millie, because he didn't want to step on Mitch's toes. In a town as small as Chestnut Springs, Travis didn't need to cause drama.

Dinner finished, and dessert was brought out. While he ate his way through a beautiful piece of chocolate cake, the speeches started. A friend of Jenna's from her job at the elementary school spoke, and Travis liked what Kim said. Then Seth's best man got up, and Travis watched Russ walk up to the microphone.

"To Seth and Jenna, whose love was written in the stars from the very beginning." He cleared his throat and glanced at the blissful couple at the head table. Travis felt bad for Russ. What a way to rub salt in his open wound. "Even if it took them a little while to realize how perfect they were for each other, I'm glad they did. Love you brother, and I love you too, Jenna." He lifted his glass of cider, and everyone in the room did the same.

Short and sweet. Exactly the kind of toast Travis appreciated.

"It's time to dance," a woman said from the mic, trilling out a laugh afterward. "Let's stand and follow Mr. and Mrs. Johnson to the dance floor."

Travis stood, steadying his father who'd broken his leg and hip in a terrible horseback riding accident a few years ago. Seth and Jenna walked by hand-in-hand, and they looked so happy that Travis could feel their joy radiating from them.

He smiled, and his heart pinched, because he was happy for them—and he wanted what they had.

The music started, and Seth took Jenna in his arms and danced with her. Then he twirled her out, where Isaac received her, dancing the father's dance in place of their father, who'd died years and years ago.

Travis clapped along with everyone else at the end of that dance, thinking he'd slip outside for a few minutes. Just to breathe and clear his head.

The dance floor was beautiful, lit with white tea lights and filled with vines and flowers. The music was low, and if there had been someone there he wanted to dance with, Travis thought it would've been the perfect place for a romantic connection.

Several more couples flooded the dance floor, including Rex and his flavor of the week. Griffin found a woman and took off his hat as he asked her to dance.

"You gonna dance?" Russ asked, and Travis shook his head.

"Who would I ask?"

"I dunno," Russ said, nodding across the room. "How about that pretty blonde over there?"

Travis followed his gaze, and he stumbled backward when he caught sight of Millie Hepworth. His heartbeat played leapfrog with itself, and he searched for Mitch. His hopes fell, because she had to be here with someone. She wasn't single.

"No," he murmured.

"Oh, go on," Russ said. "I know you like her."

"She's dating someone."

"Is she?" Russ pulled out his phone and started swiping. "I don't think so." He handed his phone to Travis, who tore his eyes away from the woman he'd been thinking about for two months to look at it.

"Going to a wedding alone tonight," he read. "Wish me luck." He looked up at Russ. "Alone?"

"I think she broke up with Anders."

So she was single. And beautiful. And standing next to her chair, a fake smile on her face as she watched everyone else dance.

"Now's your chance, Trav," Russ said, taking his phone back and nudging Travis to get moving. "Go ask her to dance."

Somehow, Travis's feet did what Russ said. His brain buzzed, because he wasn't quite sure how to talk to a woman like Millie. In fact, women like Millie had shredded his heart and left him for dead more than once. And he was willingly going to walk into that trap again?

On accident, he kicked a chair at the table beside hers, drawing her attention. Their eyes met, and it was like the entire scene around them disappeared. There were still romantic, twin-kling lights. Soft music. The scent of chocolate hanging in the air.

But now, there was only the two of them.

Travis lifted his hand for some reason. "Hey, Millie," he said. "Do you want to dance?" He should've whisked off his cowboy hat the way Griffin had done. Offered her his hand. Something.

A smile brightened her face, and she nodded, coming toward him. He did offer her his arm then, and she slipped her hand through it as he led her onto the dance floor.

Now he just had to try to dance without stepping on her feet or saying something stupid.

Totally easy, he told himself, every nerve ending in his body feeling like he'd lit it on fire. He took her into his arms, noticing how well she fit there. He breathed in and smiled.

The very next thing he did was step on her foot, and pure humiliation streamed through him. "Sorry," he muttered, putting another several inches of distance between them. Foolishness filled him, because now he was dancing like a freaking Franken-stein, his arms straight out.

"I'm not as good at this as my brother," he muttered.

Millie smiled at him, and it looked less fake than before. Still a little strained. "It's fine, Travis," she said, and wow, he liked his name in her voice.

"So you're back in town," he said, instantly regretting it. He'd said almost exactly the same thing to her at the speed dating event, almost two months ago.

"Yeah." She nodded and inched forward until they were dancing close again. "You took a long time to call," she said.

"Well, you were datin' someone else." He looked at her, surprised that he could make eye contact. "I didn't want to intrude."

The song ended, and Travis fell back a step, letting his hands drop from Millie's waist. She tucked her hair and glanced around. "Will you dance with me again?"

"Sure," Travis said, searching his mind for something they could talk about. He wasn't great with conversations, especially when they were with pretty women. He tucked her back into his arms, and they moved easily together. "So are you saying you're not dating anyone right now?" he asked.

She smiled up at him, her straight, white teeth catching some of the light from the strands around the room. "No, not right now."

"So you and Mitch…"

"Broken up," she said. She leaned her head against his shoulder, and wow, Travis sure liked that. She made him feel sexy and strong, and he closed his eyes as the song played around them.

"Uh, Trav?"

He opened his eyes at the sound of Rex's voice. Millie straightened too, and he reminded himself they were in public.

"Yeah?"

"You guys are under the mistletoe." Rex pointed up, a wicked smile on his face. "Better kiss 'er, or you'll have bad luck for a year."

Travis's heart went wild, and his feet rooted to the spot. Rex spun his woman away, and Travis had nowhere else to look but at Millie.

To his great surprise, she smiled, gripped his shoulders with a bit more strength, and closed her eyes. With her face tipped up like that, all Travis had to do to kiss her was lean down.

So he did.

CHAPTER TWO

Millie Hepworth's pulse shout out beats like an automatic machine gun. Travis Johnson was kissing her in the middle of the dance floor at his brother's wedding, and she was not complaining. Not one little bit.

She kissed him back, sliding her hands up his neck and into his hair. She'd been thinking about him for a couple of weeks now. Longer, if she were being honest with herself. But she had been dating Mitch until very recently, and Travis hadn't called...

He was certainly speaking to her right now, though, without saying a word.

He finally pulled away, dancing them away from the sprig of mistletoe hung in the very center of the light strings. "Wow," he whispered, his cheek pressed against hers.

He smelled like something musky, and something clean, and something woodsy. She liked all of it, and she couldn't get her voice to work.

"So," Travis said, obviously more relaxed now. "What are you doing here? I didn't realize you were friends with Jenna."

"Oh, I'm not," Millie said, glad her voice had decided to work again.

"So you're crashing the wedding?" He chuckled, the sound deep, rich, and delicious.

She giggled with him, surprised at how easy being with him was. Before she'd left Chestnut Springs, years ago, he'd been harder to talk to. "No, I'm not crashing," she said. "I'm shadowing Paige, and she's the wedding planner."

"Shadowing her? Why?"

"That's what I do now," she said. "I mean, not the shadowing." She sighed, because there was a very long story to how she'd come to be at this wedding, in this man's arms. "I moved home to take care of my momma, right?" She'd mentioned that during the speed dating event.

"Yeah," Travis said. "I remember that."

"So, in San Antonio, I worked for a golf course and country club, doing all of their events. I have a degree in hospitality management with a specialization in outdoor events. Up here, I've opened my own business doing the same thing. Outdoor event planning, and I've been shadowing some of the established businesses who do events."

"But this is an indoor event," Travis said, his eyebrows furrowing.

He was devilishly good-looking when he did that, and Millie smiled at him again. "True. I was just getting a sense of what a Texas Hill Country wedding would look like. I'm meeting with Serendipity Seeds on Monday to look at their space. I'm hoping to have my website done by Friday next week, and then...I'm taking on clients."

Millie felt a little bit sick to her stomach just thinking about it. But she pushed past the nerves, the butterflies, and the fear. "But the event planning gives me some flexibility with Momma, and I need that right now."

She also needed to get paid, but she kept that part buried under her tongue.

"Sounds amazing," Travis said. "My brother does dog adoptions once a month. Does that qualify as an outdoor event one might need a planner for?"

Millie laughed again and shook her head. "I don't think so, Travis."

"Hmm. He might have to do them every week the way people have been bringing him dogs."

Millie tilted her head to the side, hearing something in his voice. "You don't sound happy about that."

"He's leaving for two weeks," Travis said, glancing over to where Seth and Jenna danced, obviously hopelessly in love with one another. "And we get a few new dogs each week. We have nowhere to put them." He met Millie's eye again, and she had the inexplicable urge to want to help him.

"Do you need more housing for them?" she asked. "My mother has a huge backyard, and it's just going to waste."

"We have lots of space on the ranch," he said. "Just not the physical facilities. Seth needs to build a much bigger place."

"Maybe you should hire someone to come do it while he's gone," she suggested. "Like a wedding gift for him."

Travis looked at her, his expression thoughtful. "That's actually a good idea."

Millie smiled and tucked herself right into his personal space. "And Travis, I hope you won't wait another two months to call me again." The last notes of the music faded, this dance over. "Or for the first time." She slipped her hands down his arms and backed up one step, and then another. "I enjoyed dancing with you."

With that, Millie turned and left the dance floor. Her internal temperature could only be labeled as scorching hot, and she needed to check in with Paige anyway. She reminded herself that she was working tonight, not there to dance the night away with a sexy cowboy.

Still, she felt Travis's eyes tracking her as she wove through the tables to the exit. Once there, she turned back, but he was nowhere to be found. A sigh slipped from her mouth, and all she could do was hope and pray that he would call her this time.

TRAVIS DID NOT CALL THAT WEEKEND, BUT MILLIE TOLD herself it was because it was a holiday weekend. Her brothers had gathered for a Thanksgiving Day meal, but they each lived within a couple hours' drive of their mother, and they hadn't stayed the night.

So it was that Millie woke on Monday morning, her meeting with Serendipity Seeds still hours away. Darkness coated everything, and she was alone in the house where she'd grown up. Well, her mother was here, too, but Millie felt like she was alone.

Her mother had just turned seventy years old over the summer, and Millie hated seeing her feeble and weak. She'd always been rail thin and somewhat sickly from an autoimmune disease that she simply lived with. But she'd been diagnosed with ovarian cancer the week after her birthday, and things had gone downhill from there.

In and out of the hospital, her mother had needed help. So Millie had tied up her affairs in San Antonio, and moved the hour and a half north.

She sighed as she swung her legs over the edge of the bed. At least her mother had converted the bedrooms where her children had grown up into adult sleeping spaces. Millie had a nice queen-sized bed, with gray curtains on the windows and a desk for her business work.

But she didn't want to be alone the way she felt now. She didn't want to grow old alone, the way her mother had. She wanted a family, and children, and lots of grandchildren, and a husband that would stick with her through thick and thin.

Every time Millie thought about her father, she grew a little angry. She'd worked to overcome the feelings of abandonment he'd left her with, and she closed her eyes and breathed in deep, the way one therapist had taught her to do.

Her father had left because of something inside him, not anything to do with her. She continued to meditate, working through the feelings that seemed more prevalent in the few months since she'd returned to Chestnut Springs.

Eventually, she showered and went into the kitchen, where her mother sat nursing a cup of tea. She'd been a vegan for Millie's whole life, but when she'd been hospitalized, she'd been told that she was severely malnourished and needed to eat protein. She'd been eating small servings of chicken and fish since, and she had come out the other side of the bloating and inflammation well.

"Morning, Momma." Millie dropped a kiss on her mother's forehead. "Want to go for a walk after my meeting? We need to get in our mile."

"Yes, baby," her mother said, which is what she said to pretty much everything Millie said. She used to have beautiful, blonde hair that Millie knew she dyed to keep it the color she wanted. But since the chemotherapy treatments, she'd stopped doing that, and now her hair was a lovely shade of silver. She'd cut it too, and the natural curls made her look almost childlike.

"Did you eat breakfast?"

She lifted her teacup, and Millie suppressed a sigh. Her mother was often nauseous in the morning, but she still needed to eat. "I'll make a protein pancake, okay?"

"Okay."

Millie set to work doing that, glad they were going walking later. "All right, Momma. I have to go now."

"Knock 'em dead, baby," she said, and Millie gave her mom a warm smile. She kept her confidence as she drove over to Serendipity Seeds, but the moment she got out of her car, she felt like a shell of who she should be. Why would they want to partner with her, an event coordinator they'd never worked with before?

Because they need someone, Millie told herself. And you're good. You have a decade of experience, at a venue much more upscale than this.

She glanced around at the storefront, but she continued past it to the event center farther from the parking lot. The gardens back here would be glorious in the spring, and she really wanted to be here to see them. She wanted to plan a company party here. A wedding. A reception. The monthly meeting for the classic cars club in Gillespie County. Anything and everything.

Taking a deep breath and tugging on the bottom of her robin's egg blue jacket, she opened the door and went inside.

All they could tell her was no. Millie was used to that word, if her dating history counted. Armed with the knowledge that no wouldn't break her, she approached the woman sitting at the reception desk. "Hello, ma'am," she said. "I'm here to speak with Mildred White about the event planning coordinator position?"

She put on her most professional smile at the same time her phone rang. She didn't want to look at it, so she ignored it while the woman glanced at the large desk calendar on the desk in front of her.

Millie's fingers fumbled over the phone in her purse, silencing it with the buttons on the side.

"Millie, right?" The woman glanced up.

"Yes, ma'am."

"You can go right on back," she said. "Mildred is waiting for you."

For a terrifying moment, Millie thought she was late, but a quick glance at the clock behind the desk told her she wasn't. "Thank you." She stepped past the desk as the woman rose to open the door for her.

Once behind the safety of it, a hallway stretched for several yards, with another door waiting for her there. She quickly took out her phone, just to make sure Momma hadn't called with a dire need.

One swipe, and she saw a number she didn't recognize. So not Momma. Maybe it had been someone looking to hire her, and hope filled her chest before she could tell herself that few things were more dangerous than hope.

As she stared at the phone with a Texas area code, a text came in.

Hey, Millie. This is Travis Johnson. Call me after your meeting, would you? Sorry if I interrupted you.

The two numbers matched, and Millie's elevated pulse shot right through the roof.

He'd called. Travis Johnson had called, and Millie lifted her head high and strode toward the door at the end of the hall. Even if she didn't get this job, today was the brightest one she'd had in a long time—because Travis had called.

CHAPTER THREE

Travis shoved his phone in his pocket, feeling foolish for calling *and* texting Millie. She'd told him she had a meeting that day, but he wasn't sure when, and he hadn't thought of it until his call went to voicemail.

And then he had to text, because she didn't have his number. He only had hers. So if she didn't answer numbers she didn't know, and she wasn't in a meeting, maybe she'd call him back.

His phone stayed silent and still in his back pocket, and he turned back to Tomas, Brian, and Darren. They all wore gloves, and Travis reached for a pair as well. "Okay, let's go get the cattle moved."

They all piled into one pickup truck, with Tomas behind the wheel. The drive out to the farthest edge of the ranch was long and bumpy, and the journey back toward the epicenter would take all day as well as part of another. Moving three thousand head of cattle took forever, and Travis wished Russ had drawn the short end of the stick as far as the cattle relocation went.

The thing was, there were certain chores around the ranch that none of the brothers liked. They still had to be done, and Travis had drawn the cattle this go-round. He'd move them in closer to the center of the ranch for the rainy winter, and hopefully, someone else would have to move them back out once spring came.

Russ would have his hands full with the animals as it was, including all of the dogs, horses, goats, chickens, and pigs. And while December was right around the corner, everything from the front gate, around Seth's Canine Encounters, and back to the storage shed at the edge of the yard needed to be mowed back for the winter.

So Russ had plenty to do as well. Rex and Griffin would come out and scrub all of the stables, as well as all the feed and water troughs. Maybe they'd drawn the short stick, and Travis smiled to himself as he looked out the passenger window.

His mind had been circling Millie Hepworth for days now, and he hated that he was driving out into the wilds of the Texas Hill Country without talking to her first. He'd gone out with her several times over a decade ago, and he'd liked her then.

He was a different person now, and he was sure she was too. He just needed some time to find out.

"I love this song," Brian said, reaching out to turn the radio up. He loved anything with guitars and country twang, about how the love of one's life had walked out the door. Brian grinned as he started singing along, and Travis chuckled at him. Brian, Tomas, and Darren had been living and working at Chestnut Ranch since Seth had come back full-time, and they'd been a huge help.

Travis had worked with them the most, as he was in charge of the agriculture on the ranch, and it was a big job to prep fields, plant them, rotate them irrigate them, and then harvest them. It sure seemed like the fields just grew themselves, but Travis knew there was so much more behind farming.

And he loved it.

His phone buzzed near the end of the song, and he shifted to pull it out of his back pocket. He didn't want to hope the message could be from Millie, but well, he really hoped it was.

A smile burst onto his face when he saw her name on the screen. I called but it went right to voicemail. Call me when you have service?

Travis checked his bars, and he only had two. They'd probably driven through a patch of better service, and her text had come through. *Sure,* he tapped out. *I'm moving cattle today, but there's usually service at the cabin.*

He tapped the arrow to send it, but the circle just spun and spun. The text wouldn't go through, and frustration built inside him. *Sorry, the service is bad on some parts of the ranch.*

He and Russ and Seth had talked about it before, but there was nothing they could do. Well, they could buy a cell phone tower, but those were super-expensive.

And you're a billionaire, he thought. Sometimes he forgot he had a lot of money now. He'd taken his father's advice and not spent a dime. Well, besides a truck. He'd *needed* that, though.

His texts went through, and he grinned at his phone.

"Who are you talking to?" Brian asked, glancing at Travis.

"No one," he said, flipping his phone over.

"Oh, I see how it is." Brian grinned at him. "Must be a woman."

"Who?" Tomas asked, leaning forward.

"He said no one," Darren said. "Didn't you hear him?"

"I've decided I'm going to ask out Lucy McBride," Tomas said, not an ounce of embarrassment in his voice.

"Yeah?" Brian asked. "Because you know she's semi-crazy, right?" He laughed, and it was good-natured.

"I heard that too," Darren said.

"In what way?" Tomas asked, and Travis was just glad they weren't badgering him about who he was texting.

"She loves the full moon," Brian said. "The rumors are that she does a little dance every month, claiming it's good luck."

"I like the moon," Tomas said, and Brian and Darren burst out laughing. Travis joined in, because he wasn't sure about dancing under the moon either.

He did remember that Millie liked doing things outside.

Hiking and rafting and all that kind of stuff. Travis didn't mind being outside sometimes, but the heat in Texas could be oppressive in the summer. Thankfully, he had a few more months before he had to deal with off-the-charts temperatures again.

His phone buzzed, and he flipped it over so fast he almost threw it into Brian's lap. But Millie had said, *No problem. Would love to chat when you get somewhere with service.*

He hurried to send her a thumbs-up before he lost service— and before Brian could see. Yes, he needed service, but he also needed privacy.

HE, BRIAN, TOMAS, AND DARREN WORKED WELL TOGETHER, and they made it to the cabin with the cattle about an hour before nightfall. As Brian set to work getting dinner going, Travis managed to excuse himself and find a spot on the front porch away from the other two men.

The scent of grass and horses and cows filled the air, and Travis took a deep breath of it. He sure did love ranching. The faint scent of wood smoke grew, and he heard Brian laugh from the back of the cabin, where he'd put something over the fire for them to eat.

Travis focused on his phone. Millie had texted a few more times, and he liked that she seemed as into starting a relationship with him as he felt about having one with her.

A relationship.

Travis took a deep breath and looked out over the fields in front of him. "I can't believe you're doing this," he said, as if he was two halves of a whole. The part that didn't want to be alone anymore lifted the phone back into his eyesight.

She'd mentioned what she was doing that day and had asked him more about what it took to move cattle. He could type it all out, but Travis decided to call instead.

The half of him that had been scarred by pretty blondes like Millie wailed, but the ringing of her phone drowned that out.

"Hey," she said, her voice happy and bright.

A bit of that light leaked into Travis's soul, and he smiled. "Hey, there." Problem was, he didn't have much to say after that.

Thankfully, Millie said, "Do you have time for a story?"

"Definitely," he said.

"So I went to Serendipity Seeds today, right?"

"Right." He could sure get used to just saying one-word answers.

"Do you know Mildred White?"

"No, ma'am." Seth probably did, but then again, Seth left the ranch more often than Travis did.

"Well, she's kind of intimidating, and she's like my mother's age." Millie laughed, and it added more of that bright light to Travis's soul. "Anyway, the interview was with her, and I thought it went okay...until the end."

"Uh oh," he said. "What happened at the end?"

"She asked me if I had any experience planning bachelor parties."

Travis couldn't wait to hear if Millie did or not. "And?" he prompted when she didn't continue.

"I worked at a golf course," she said. "Country club. There were *plenty* of bachelor parties."

"Oh, so easy answer," he said, wondering what she thought of such events.

"I thought so, too," she said. "Then Mildred kept firing questions at me about how I'd plan a bachelor party for a guy who loved fishing and whittling and the scenario was so specific, I asked her if Serendipity had a bachelor party already on the books she wanted me to do." She laughed again, and she couldn't stop. "And she finally..." She couldn't speak through her laughter. "Said it was her fiancé's bachelor party."

"Oh, wow." Travis chuckled too. "But hey, everyone deserves love, right?"

That got her to sober right up, and Travis wondered if he'd said something wrong.

"Right," she said. "I just thought it was funny. She doesn't want to plan his bachelor party, but she definitely does."

"So are you gonna do it?" Travis asked.

"Yes," Millie said, a hint of pride entering her voice. "Because you're talking to the newest addition to the Serendipity Seeds family. I got the contract!"

"That's great, sugar," he drawled, really happy for her. Number one, it would keep her in town. And number two, he wanted her to stay in town for a good, long while. "Are you still going to run your own business?"

"Yep," Millie said. "The event coordinator at Serendipity has some very slow times. For example, all of the Christmas stuff is already done, so I'm not really going to be doing much until the New Year anyway. Even then, all I do is make sure the different events at the farm are scheduled and our staff is ready."

Travis's mind started revolving, but he didn't blurt out what he was thinking. He should probably at least talk to Russ about having a family Christmas party at the homestead before he hired Millie.

Maybe.

Or maybe he should just do it. They'd been going to his parents' on Victory Street for the holidays for the past several years, but Travis really wanted to have some traditions back on the ranch.

He'd loved growing up out there, and his mother had put the "home" in "homestead."

Despite his claims to the contrary, Seth had been broken when he'd returned to the homestead. Travis had been living there already, and he'd done the best he could when Russ and Seth moved in. But that meant they all went into town and let their mother feed them for birthdays and holidays.

After a while, they'd started playing games and having treats on Sunday afternoons and evenings, and Travis really liked that.

But with Seth gone…he wondered if his brother and his new wife would come over to the homestead on Sundays. He sure hoped so.

"So," Millie said. "Do you have any funny stories from today?"

Travis thought about her question. "Do you think moving cattle is funny?"

She giggled. "I mean, maybe something happened that was funny."

"Not really," he said, wondering if he'd be exciting enough for Millie. "I mean, there was this cow that tried to disappear up into the trees, and I had to go after it. Then it just stood there and stared at me like I was the one doin' something wrong."

She giggled again, and Travis did like the addition of her laugh to his life. "Cows are stubborn things."

"They sure are, sweetheart."

"You're moving them?"

"Yep, closer in so we don't have to go out as far in the rainy parts of winter."

"When will you be back?"

"Tomorrow afternoon." He cleared his throat. "What do you think about going to dinner with me tomorrow night?"

CHAPTER FOUR

A grin burst across Millie's face, and she looked up at the ceiling. She'd thought Travis would never ask her out, and yet, there the words were, still ringing in her ears.

"Dinner sounds great," she said. She'd really been treating herself today, and with a date on the horizon tomorrow, everything had just gotten better. A new job, a new boyfriend...

Millie tried not to get ahead of herself.

"Where do you like to eat?" he asked.

"Oh, I like food," she said, trying not to move too much. She was currently soaking in the tub—another real treat for her—and she didn't want Travis to know. She also didn't want to drop her phone in the bubbly water. Now *that* would be a real tragedy, seeing as how it had taken this man two months to call her.

Yes, she'd been dating Mitch. So Travis was a gentleman for not bullying his way into her life. A real cowboy gentleman—who made her heartbeat flutter.

"Well, you pick," he said. "I don't want to pick. I like food too."

"What do you feel like?" she asked.

"I have no idea," he said, his words carrying a smile. "It's tomorrow."

"What are you eating tonight?"

"Uh, let's see. Smells like steak."

"So no steak tomorrow." She really liked talking to him. "But maybe you are the type of man that could eat the same thing twice in a row."

"As long as I don't have to cook it, I'm fine with anything."

"Can you cook, Mister Johnson?" Oh, flirting with him was even better, and Millie wished she was with him wherever he was right now.

"I mean, I'm thirty-five years old and haven't died yet," he said, chuckling.

"Yeah, but does your mother feed you every night?"

"Not *every* night," he said.

Millie burst out laughing, glad when Travis joined in. There was the relaxed, laid-back cowboy she'd met ten years ago. Well, before that, if she were being honest. They'd both grown up in Chestnut Springs, but they hadn't run in the same social circles in high school. Her mother was exceptionally good at knowing all the gossip, especially about old families in town, and Millie knew Seth had gone off to college and not finished, and that Russ had entered the Army after high school.

Travis was two years older than her in school, and he'd left Chestnut Springs too. Off to college was the rumor, but she hadn't asked her mother if he'd finished. She wanted to learn about Travis from Travis, and she could hardly wait until tomorrow night for dinner.

"You still there?" he asked, and Millie focused on the reality in front of her. She hated gossip anyway.

"Yes," she said. "I'm thinking I'm going to feel like a big salad tomorrow night." She waited to see how he'd react to that, but he said nothing. That was an improvement over Mitch's groan and eye-rolling every time she wanted a salad for dinner.

"There's the soup place," he said. "They have good salads...I think."

"You don't actually eat salad, right?" she asked.

"I mean, if my mom makes it," he said. "Or Seth or Russ. They do most of the cooking around the homestead. I guess just Russ now. Seth moved out."

Millie tried to hear how he felt about that, but then reminded herself that she didn't have to analyze every little thing to death. She could be detail-oriented and organized in her event planning. She didn't need to turn into Sigmund Freud on Travis Johnson.

"You're right, though," she said. "The Cauldron has great soups and salads."

"The Cauldron?" he asked. "Is it really called that?"

"Has been for twenty years, Travis." She giggled again, really wishing she wouldn't. She cut the sound short only to hear him chuckling too.

"This might be a funny story," he said. "One of the guys I'm working with, he's going to ask out this woman who likes to dance under the full moon."

"Oh, Lucy McBride," Millie said, and that got Travis laughing even harder.

"How'd you know?" he asked.

"Everyone knows about Lucy," Millie said. "She's a little…crazy."

"That's what Brian said," Travis said. "Do you think she is really? I mean, maybe I should tell Tomas before he asks her out."

"Do you guys talk a lot about your dates?" Millie asked.

"No," he said quickly. "I mean, it helps that I never date."

"Never? What's tomorrow night then?"

"Almost never," he clarified. "And tomorrow night is…"

Millie waited, her breath held in her chest. It felt like whatever Travis said was going to define their relationship, and they hadn't even gone out yet.

"I'm really looking forward to tomorrow night," he finally said.

"Me too," Millie said, wanting to squeal but holding it in. "See you then."

"Yep, see you."

She hung up and set her phone on the tub-side tray she used to hold her toiletries. Then she slid under the water and let out that squeal. That way, Momma wouldn't hear, and Millie could keep her and Travis's budding new relationship a secret for just a little longer.

A delicious, handsome cowboy, secret.

"Come on, Momma," Millie said the next morning. "Time to get up." It was actually about two hours past time to get up, and still her mother lay in bed.

"I don't feel good today," she said, still facing the window.

"I know," Millie said, trying to be strong and soft at the same time. "But the doctor wants you out of bed every day. We need to take our walk." And she had paperwork to sign at Serendipity, and then she needed plenty of time to get ready for her date. Not only that, but she'd need to feed Momma before she left, and she hadn't even told her about the dinner with Travis yet.

Her mother didn't move, and Millie sighed as she fully entered the bedroom. She hated being in here, because the air was musty and un-recycled, and her mother refused to let Millie open a window. She had to pick her battles, because she couldn't win them all.

"What hurts?" she asked, feeling very much like the roles between her and her mom had been reversed. She could distinctly remember when her mother had come into her room when Millie was a teenager and didn't want to go to school. She'd asked the same question then.

"My head," her mom said. "My chest. My back."

"I'll reheat the tea," Millie said. "And bring it to you with some pain medication. Okay?" She reached out but stopped short of touching her mother. A fierce love for the woman moved through her though, and she got up without waiting for her mom to respond.

In the kitchen, Millie opened the window and basked in the fresh air. She set the tea kettle on the stove and started typing out a text to her brothers. She wished they felt a little more responsibility to help out, but she didn't live their lives. Two of them were married with kids, and the third had a stressful job quite the drive away.

Millie had moved home specifically to have time to help her mother through moments like this. And David, Chris, and Rick were supportive, as they each responded almost instantly to her update about their mother.

I'll send dinner tonight, David said.

I'm so sorry, Chris said. Call me if she won't get up in ten minutes, and I'll call her.

You're the best, Mills, Rick said. I can get out there this weekend if you need a day off.

Tears came to her eyes at the love and support from her older brothers. She couldn't judge them, and she didn't resent them.

She would like a day off, though. And what kind of daughter did that make her? She'd only been home for two and a half months. Still, she did provide day-in and day-out care for her mom, and she was exhausted. It was the not-knowing she didn't like. Yesterday, her mother had beat her to the kitchen, the tea already in her hand by the time Millie had made an appearance.

And tonight, her mom could throw a fit when Millie prepared to leave.

Dinner would be awesome, she sent to her brothers. I have a date tonight, and it might help me get out of the house more easily.

Do not tell me you're going out with Mitch again, Chris sent back.

And I'd love a day off this weekend, Rick, she sent, ignoring Chris's message—for now. Even just a couple of hours to get my hair done.

I'll be there Saturday by noon, her brother said. I'll bring the kids, and you can go do whatever you want. Who's the date with? (Please don't say Mitch.)

You know who you should go out with? David sent, and Millie muttered, "Here we go." How was it that the single brother thought he could advise her on who she dated?

Who? she typed out anyway.

One of those Johnson boys, he sent back. *Remember them? Chestnut Ranch?*

Millie started laughing, because the whole situation was just too ironic.

Seth was my age, David said.

Seth got married, Chris said. I think Griffin is your age, Mills.

"It's actually Travis," she said as she typed the same words. She hesitated before sending them though. But her brothers would find out anyway, and Millie needed to tell Momma too. Maybe if she told her now, her mother wouldn't have a reason to prevent Millie from going later.

She sent the text and added, and we're going to dinner tonight. So good call, Davy.

With her brothers' texts coming in fast and furious still, Millie poured the hot water over the tea bag and stirred it absently. Her brothers wouldn't discourage her from dating Travis—and they only didn't like Mitch because of what she'd told them.

While the tea steeped, she looked at her phone again. She'd been right, and all of the messages were positive and said things like, *Let us know how it goes* or *I can't wait to hear how it went.*

Okay, she said. *Going to check on Momma again.*

And she did just that, finding her mother sitting up in bed. *Baby steps,* she thought as she entered the room again and handed her mother the teacup.

"You're such a good girl, Millie," she said, sighing as she sipped her tea.

"Momma." She sat on the edge of the bed again. "I have a date tonight."

"You're seeing Mitch again?"

"No," Millie said. "Travis Johnson."

Her mother's eyes widened. "Wow, Millie. He's a great catch."

"It's our first date, Momma." She shook her head and smiled. "And I don't want the whole town to know."

"I won't tell a soul," she said, though the news had definitely perked her up. Millie also didn't believe her, but maybe her mother thought her friends were soulless.

"He's coming at five-thirty," she said. "I'll let you meet him if you've showered and promise to be on your best behavior."

Her mother set her teacup on the bedside table and flung the covers off her legs. "I'll shower right now."

Millie grinned at her mom and helped steady her. "Great. Yell at me if you need anything."

She left her mother alone in the bathroom, glad she'd been able to get her out of bed. But what would she use next time to motivate her mother to do what she needed to do?

An alarm sounded on her phone, and she startled. "Shoot," she muttered under her breath. She'd completely forgotten about the conference call with Gillian Donnelly, a woman whose son was supposed to be getting engaged very soon.

She saw more texts from her brothers too, and a couple from Travis too. But she literally had ten minutes to be ready for a meeting she'd forgotten about, and she hurriedly pulled the elastic from her hair so she wouldn't look like she'd just rolled out of bed.

Travis would keep, and she hoped next time she spoke to him, she could tell him she'd landed her first job as an independent event planner.

CHAPTER FIVE

Travis looked at himself in the mirror, wishing Rex and Griffin hadn't made it a special event that he'd moved the cattle. He supposed he had put up a bit of a fuss over it, and his brothers had been waiting at the homestead with their mother's homemade root beer and plenty of pizza.

He was stuffed to the gills already, and he hadn't even left to pick up Millie yet. He looked at himself in the mirror, deciding he looked good enough. The collar of his shirt didn't quite lay flat, but he wasn't about to get out an iron to fix it.

He hadn't shaved for a little over a week now, and he rather liked the beard that was growing in. He'd decided to keep it for now, though come Thursday night, his mother's nagging might change his mind.

"Go live like a champion," he said to his reflection, something his father had said to him many times growing up.

His nerves had been fueling his heartbroken side all day, but he left the bathroom connected to his and Russ's room and went downstairs, his cowboy boots making too much noise to escape the house without detection. And of course, it had to be Rex who came out of the kitchen to see what Travis was up to.

He whistled and said, "Hoo boy, where are you off to?"

That question brought everyone else out of the kitchen, and Travis wouldn't be able to keep his date a secret now. He ran his hands through his hair and plucked his cowboy hat from the rack beside the front door. His working hats all hung by the back door, but his dress hat had a special spot out here.

"I'm goin' out with Millie."

Rex grinned like Travis had said he'd found a cure for the hoof disease their cattle got every blasted winter. "Good for you, bro." He was only five years younger than Travis, but Travis felt like they came from different planets sometimes.

"You look like you're going to throw up," Griffin said.

"Go," Russ said, stepping in front of the younger brothers. "Don't listen to them. Have fun." He smiled at Travis and nodded as if he already knew how the date would go, and it had been good.

"What if—?"

"Nope," Russ said. "Now where are your keys?"

Travis patted his pockets, because he thought he'd put them there. But he couldn't feel them. "Shoot. I must've left them upstairs." He bolted back that way, ready to be free from the homestead. Away from the six eyes watching him. Now he'd be late, too.

He swiped the keys from the top of his dresser and headed back downstairs, feeling a bit rushed and sweaty now.

"Have fun," Russ said, and Travis lifted his hand in a wave and left his three brothers standing in the doorway that led into the kitchen.

He was so nervous he'd forgotten to say thanks for the pizza, and he'd forgotten he'd parked in the garage. He keyed in the code, which took another few seconds, and by the time he sat behind the wheel, he just wanted to go back inside. He could put on his pajamas and catch up on the sleep he'd lost last night.

The cabin out in the pastures was warm enough, and he'd eaten like a king. Brian didn't snore, Tomas only muttered in his sleep sometimes, and Darren always had the best snacks. The cots were comfortable enough. At least they'd never bothered Travis before.

What had kept him awake was this date with Millie. "Might as well get it over with," he muttered, hoping it would go better than he was imagining. And if it didn't...well, there was always next October and the speed dating event.

He drove to the address she'd texted, arriving a few minutes before he'd said he'd pick her up. So he wasn't late at all. He rotated his shoulders and fixed his denim jacket as he walked up the front sidewalk, and he drew in a long breath and held it.

Then he rang the doorbell.

Only a few seconds passed before a woman opened the door. Mostly made of skin and bones, she smiled at Travis. "Travis Johnson," she said like they were old friends.

"Ma'am." He lifted his cowboy hat in greeting.

"Oh, how polite."

"You can thank my momma," he said with a smile. "It's good to see you, Miss Hepworth." He glanced behind her, but he didn't want to be rude or seem too eager. "Should I come in?"

"Don't make him stand on the porch, Momma," Millie called from the depths of the house, and her mother stepped back. Travis entered the place, and it felt a lot like his grandmother's house. Old carpet on the floor, with obvious spots where people walked. The furniture looked a bit droopy, and the whole house needed to be aired out.

Houses this old were segmented, cut up, and he stood in a living room with a television and a recliner that had definitely seen better days. His parents had a smaller house now too, but it was newer than this place, and had been renovated before they'd bought it and moved from the ranch and to town.

He kept his smile on his face, because he didn't want Millie's mother to know what he was thinking. But honestly, he thought this place should be torn down and started from scratch.

A cat meowed and rubbed against his legs, and he looked down at it.

"Oh, don't mind Puddles," Mrs. Hepworth said. "She's declawed and mostly blind. So, Travis," she continued as if she didn't need to breathe like normal humans. "Tell me: what are you doing these days?"

"Working the ranch, ma'am."

"Is that all?"

Travis looked at her, his defenses flying right into place. "Yep," he said, because she obviously hadn't meant to insult him. But running a ranch was hard work. So hard that everything they needed to do barely got done with seven men working full time. "What are you doin' these days?" he asked, instantly regretting the question.

The woman was obviously sick, and he didn't need to cause her to drum up bad memories of being in the hospital. Heat filled his face, and he shifted his feet, but she said, "Oh, a little of this and a little of that. I like to waste a day or two at the library or the community center."

"Yeah?" He had no idea what someone would do at the community center, and his face must've shown it.

"They do some sitting aerobics for the elderly," she said.

"Oh, you're not elderly," he said, though he honestly had no idea how old Millie's mom was. He knew she had older brothers, three of 'em.

"Oh, you." Mrs. Hepworth gave a light laugh, and thankfully, Millie emerged from the kitchen. She stole Travis's attention from her mother, and he found his mouth dry and his mind blank as she approached him.

She wore a pretty pink dress with black heels that brought her closer to his height. She'd put something sparkly on her eyelids and her lips, and she slipped her arm through his as effortlessly as if she'd done it a thousand times before.

"Ready?" she asked.

"Yeah," he said, promptly clearing his throat. "Yes, I'm ready." He nodded at her mother. "Ma'am."

Mrs. Hepworth twittered again, and Millie stepped over to

the couch, where she picked up a black jacket and handed it to him. Travis managed to help her put it on, and they headed out.

Once the front door closed, Millie let out a breath. "You made her whole night."

"Did I?"

"She's been talking about you for hours," Millie said with a smile. "I think she's expecting a report when you drop me off."

Travis laughed, because he really didn't want to be thinking about her mom when he dropped Millie off later. "I think you pass."

"Do I?" She twirled at the bottom of the steps, sending her skirt into a flare.

"Definitely." He took her hand in his, remembering that kiss from last week. Four days ago. Had it really only been four days? Time had a way of lengthening into much longer segments.

He helped Millie into his truck and got behind the wheel. "Wow, Travis," she said. "This thing is really nice."

"Thanks."

"Chestnut Ranch must be doing really well."

Travis cut her a glance out of the corner of his eye. He hadn't anticipated telling her about his bank account that night. He'd never told Flora, and he didn't know how a woman would react to the word *billionaire*.

She watched him as he backed out of her driveway. "It's okay," she said. "That was a pretty rude thing to ask anyway."

"What did you ask?"

"How much you make." She shook her head and glanced down at her folded hands. "I'm sorry. It's none of my business. I mean, I wouldn't like it if you asked me that."

"Noted," he said. "How was your conference call?"

"Uh, it went okay," she said, her voice pitching up. Which meant it hadn't gone as well as she would've liked. Travis had learned a lot about humans from observing them for so long.

"I'm sorry," he said. "Maybe they just need to think about it?"

"Maybe," she said. "Gillian doesn't even know when the engagement will happen."

"Makes it hard to plan, then," he said. "And even harder to hire an event planner."

Millie giggled, and Travis smiled, glad she wasn't too upset about the job she hadn't gotten. "Right?"

Travis searched his brain for something else to talk about. He didn't want their relationship to be about work. "So we've been out before," he said. "But I imagine ten years changes a woman. Tell me one thing that's the same about you and one thing that's different."

"Oh, I like this game. Will you do it too?"

"Sure," he said, navigating them toward downtown Chestnut Springs.

"Okay, let's see." Millie exhaled as if he'd asked her something really hard. "I still love pistachio ice cream."

"Oh, yeah," he said, smiling. "I remember that. It's not good, by the way. The ice cream."

"Bite your tongue," she teased, and Travis reached over and took her hand in his again. This was easier than he'd thought it would be. And he liked easy.

"One thing that's different...I'm a cat person now."

"Ouch," he said. "That's a hard one to swallow."

"You're a dog person." She wasn't asking.

"Guilty," he said. "We only have cats at the ranch to keep the mice under control."

"See? They're useful. What do the dogs do for you?"

"They love you unconditionally," he said, realizing too late that he'd given away much more than he'd wanted to. He cleared his throat and looked at Millie again. She gaped openly at him now.

"Travis...have you been hurt?"

"Hurt?" he repeated. Memories from the past ten years flashed through his mind, one image after the other, quick as lightning. He pulled into The Cauldron and parked before looking at Millie.

"I'm going to tell you this anyway," he said. "Maybe I wasn't planning on doing it tonight, but…" He cleared his throat again, telling himself to *stop doing that*.

Millie didn't pressure him or demand he tell her. He really liked that. He really liked her, and he wanted to learn to trust women again.

He opened his mouth and said, "Yes, Millie. I've had a string of girlfriends—one who was a fiancée—who've taught me that having a good dog who's always happy to see you is really important."

CHAPTER SIX

"Wow." Millie said the first thing that came to her mind. "A fiancée."

"*Ex*-fiancée," he said. "At least she broke it off before I was standing at the altar."

Shock moved through Millie. "I'm sorry, Trav." His nickname simply came out of her mouth, and she flinched. Travis didn't seem to care at all. His dark eyes burned with an intensity he'd always possessed. That look made him hot and mysterious to Millie, and she wanted to unravel every piece of this man, lay them out, and examine them individually.

"It's okay," he said. "But you're the first—okay, second—woman I've been out with in a while."

"How long?"

"Uh, let's see. Probably four years or so."

He'd been caged at Chestnut Ranch for four years. No wonder her mother didn't know much gossip about him. "Who else did you go out with?"

"Flora Thompson." He whisked off his cowboy hat and ran his hand up the back of his head before reseating his hat. "She said there were no sparks."

Millie didn't see how that was even possible. Travis emitted electricity as if he was made of only charged particles. His own personal electrical storm. "Wow," she said, shaking her head.

Travis had started to get out of the truck, and he said, "I'll come around."

She watched him round the hood and come open her door. Smiling down at him, Millie slipped her hand into his and dropped to the ground, her skirt fluttering around her knees.

"What does wow mean?" he asked, not giving her a single inch to breathe air that wasn't scented with his woodsy cologne.

"What does *wow* mean?" she repeated.

"Yeah, I said there were no sparks between me and Flora, and you said wow."

"Oh, it was like wow, I don't see how that's possible." She reached up and cupped her hand around Travis's bearded jaw. Flutters started in her stomach and a shower of sparks moved down her spine. "Yep, plenty of sparks."

Travis held her gaze easily, and Millie could melt under the heat in those eyes. "For me too," he whispered, and for one insanely wonderful moment, Millie thought he'd kiss her again.

Instead, he backed up a step, cleared his throat again, and said, "I'm starving," in a voice that also gave away how nervous he was.

Millie ducked her head and tucked her wavy hair behind one ear. "Me too," she said.

"I just lied," he said with a shaky laugh. "My brothers brought out pizza for dinner tonight, and I didn't tell them about our date until after I'd eaten." He looked at her again, and he looked half-angry and half-apologetic.

"You didn't tell them we were going out?"

"Oh, no, they know," he said. "I couldn't get out of the house in a button-up shirt without them knowing." He chuckled, and Millie added her laughter to his. "I just…I'm trying not to screw up too badly here."

"You're doin' fine," she said, squeezing his hand. "More than fine." They entered the restaurant, and Travis stepped over to the hostess station.

The woman there grabbed two menus and said, "Follow me, please."

Millie and Travis's conversation stalled while they walked through the restaurant and settled into a booth with a globe above the table that cast romantic light onto them.

"Okay," Millie said as she picked up her menu. "Your turn."

"For what?"

"One thing that's the same, and one that's different."

Travis grinned at her. "Okay, that's easy. I still love horses and dogs and ranching. And as for what's different…I actually like salad."

Millie burst out laughing, and Travis grinned at her with a new sparkle in his eyes. She reasoned that the other woman he'd been out with must've been braindead, because the attraction between her and Travis was off the charts—and she couldn't wait to kiss him again.

"Do y'all know what you'd like?"

Millie glanced up at the waitress, but the woman only looked at Travis. He didn't seem to notice as he ordered a kale and rice barbecue bowl. He looked over at her, and still Little Miss didn't look at Millie.

She popped her gum and stared at Travis with a goofy little smile on her face.

"I'll have the corn chowder," Millie almost yelled. The woman flinched and finally looked at her. "And the large Cobb salad."

"Be right back," she chirped.

"Can we get drinks?" Travis asked, and she came flouncing back. Millie ducked her head and looked toward the condiments against the wall. Her smile couldn't be contained, and Travis said, "We want sweet tea, right, baby?"

"Mm hm," she said, trying not to laugh.

"Two sweet teas," he said, and the woman walked away again. Millie started giggling, and she couldn't stop.

"*Baby*," she said, really drawing out the word. "I think she thought you were *handsome*." She grinned at him, enjoying the flush as it crawled up his neck and into his face. "I mean, she couldn't even look at me." She really wished she had a cold iced tea in front of her, as she needed something to cool down her internal temperature as well.

"I don't mean anything by the pet names," he said. "My momma calls everyone she meets baby or sugar or sweetie."

"Yeah, I know," she said, though a pinch started behind her lungs. "I grew up in Texas too."

"Small town Texas," he said, smiling at her. "I do love Chestnut Springs. That's something that hasn't changed."

"But you did leave town," she said.

"Yes, I did."

Millie leaned into her elbows on the table. "You're really going to make me work for it, aren't you?"

"You want to know what I did when I left town."

"Yes, I do."

"Goes both ways?"

"Sure."

"I became a master carpenter," he said. "I mean, that's just a coined term, but I went to work as an apprentice under Josiah Forton, and I learned how to make cabinets as well as scaffolding, trim, and framing."

"I like a man who's good with his hands."

The waitress arrived and set down the two glasses of sweet tea, and Millie immediately reached for hers. "How long did it take to learn all of that?"

"Years," he said. "Six or seven. I worked at the cabinetry for the longest. Worked for a builder for a year or so. Came back to the ranch."

Millie liked the sound of his voice, and she hoped they'd be able to see a lot of each other in the future. "Why'd you come back to the ranch?"

"I wanted to," he said. "And my dad wanted me to build a new stable, and I fell in love with the ranch and the land all over again." He smiled over the top of his glass of sweet tea. "So I came back. I was only working over in Concan, so it wasn't a huge drive." He shrugged. "But I came back here, because...well, the fiancée became an ex, and it seemed like a good time to move."

He set his glass down and lifted his eyebrows, clearly cowboy code for *your turn, baby*.

"I went to college," she said. "UTSA. I graduated with a degree in hospitality management, emphasis on outdoor events. I came home for a month or two—that's when we dated a little —and then I started working for Fox Hill Golf Course and Country Club, where I've been for the last ten years."

"Did you like your job?" he asked.

"Yes," Millie said, smiling despite herself. "Yes, I sure did."

"And you came back to help your momma."

Her smile slipped, because Travis looked so serious, and her momma's illness was serious too. "Yes." She ground her voice through her throat. "Yes, I did."

Travis reached across the table and covered both of her hands with his. "How's she doing?"

Millie felt braver in his presence, and her heart skipped every other beat with his skin touching hers. "You know what? It's not great most days."

"I'm sorry," he said. "She hasn't lost her manners."

"Oh, my momma will die with the word *please* on her lips." Millie gave a light laugh and noticed the waitress coming with their food. Sure enough, their salads and soups got set down, and Millie admired her colorful salad. They ate in silence for a few minutes, and Millie knew Travis was a man of few words. Sometimes the silence made her uncomfortable, but this one didn't.

"Millie, I wanted to ask you something," he said, and he

looked and sounded serious. Gone was the playful, teasing Travis, and she liked both sides of him.

She took a big bite of salad and watched him. "It's about...a party. A Christmas party. A family Christmas party. At the ranch." He kept his head down, and whether he was embarrassed or not, Millie wasn't sure.

"You want me to plan a family Christmas party for the Johnsons at Chestnut Ranch?" The very idea had every cell in her body vibrating.

"Yes, that's it," he said.

He was a man of more questions than answers, but Millie rather liked that about him. "I find it hard to believe your family doesn't have a dozen traditions."

"My mother does," he said. "Those of us at the ranch don't. Not really." He pushed his fork around his bowl, not really eating. "I'd like to do a couple of things this year."

"Do you have a tree set up already?" she asked.

"No," he said.

Excitement built inside her. "There's almost nothing I like more than decorating a Christmas tree."

"That's just crazy talk," Travis said, those eyes dancing again.

"Yeah?" She leaned forward. "You want to see my brand of crazy tomorrow night?"

"Does it involve a full moon?"

Millie tipped her head back and laughed. She hadn't had such a great first date in a long, long time. "Not even a little bit," she said. "Just a great big star."

"Oh, well, stars I can handle," he said. "We might even be able to dance under the stars."

Millie took a spoonful of soup, watching him. "Don't make promises you can't keep, cowboy."

"I can keep it."

"Can you? Don't you live with your brothers?" She cocked her right eyebrow and watched his face light up.

"I'll make sure Russ is scarce tomorrow night," he said.

"Will there be mistletoe?" Millie asked, feeling a little bit wild.

Travis coughed and put his fork down. "We currently don't have any mistletoe on the ranch."

"Hmm." Millie stirred her soup, but she didn't take another bite. "I'll bring some."

Travis shook his head and chuckled. "You know, I'm not even sure what I just agreed to."

"You just booked the best event planner in the Texas Hill Country." She grinned at him, and enjoyed the deep-throated chuckle that made a flush fill her whole body.

Now she just had to figure out where to buy mistletoe with less than twenty-four hours notice.

CHAPTER SEVEN

Travis finished his coffee as Russ stood up and reached for his cowboy hat. "Russ, I need to talk to you."

"Let's talk while we feed dogs," his brother said. "And... I have something to tell you too."

Travis put his plate in the sink. "You go first."

"After you left last night, someone stopped by with another dog."

"You have got to be kidding me," Travis said, his day getting worse and it wasn't even dawn yet.

Russ stepped out the back door and held it for Travis. Their eyes met as he passed Russ, and he sensed something big was about to happen. "What?" Travis asked.

"It was Janelle."

"Oh...wow." Travis didn't know what else to say. Russ and Janelle had been seeing each other for a couple of months before she'd mysteriously broken up with him. "Did she...? Well, what did she want?"

They started walking across the lawn to the shed with the ranch trucks. "She took the dog home with her, and she offered to take six more."

"That's interesting," Travis said. "Does she have room for six abandoned dogs at her place? Because let's face it. Six dogs is a lot to feed. A lot to exercise. A lot to house. And these aren't the calmest canines on the planet." Travis loved dogs, and he thought he could charm even the most rabid one.

But the real dog whisperer was Seth, and he could actually get the excitable dogs to behave. He trained them to sit and lay down, shake and come when he called them. He spoke to them in Italian and German, and they followed him around like he was a god. To them, he was.

So while Russ and Travis could enter the canine encampment and feed and water the dogs, put them out onto the range and bring them back in, they didn't train the dogs. Seth had a very specific set of rules a dog had to meet and follow before he took them to the park for adoptions.

"She's got a barn with stalls in it," Russ said. "I've seen it, and it would work in a pinch."

"We're overflowing here," Travis said, glancing at his brother. "You don't seem too happy about her offer."

"Yeah, well, I don't trust her."

"Didn't she find a box full of puppies?"

"Yeah," Russ said.

"Maybe she's finding dogs left and right so she has a reason to see you." Travis grinned at Russ, who just shook his head.

"If she wanted to see me, all she had to do was not break-up with me."

"She must've had a reason." Travis spoke quietly, so as to not scare Russ away from talking. They got in the truck, and Russ started over to Canine Encounters. They'd spend a couple of hours there—at least—feeding and watering, moving dogs outside and cleaning out pens. Now that they had to share, things got messier much more quickly.

"She did," Russ said. "But I don't want to talk about it."

"Okay, fair enough," Travis said, though his curiosity did plague him.

"So what did you want to talk about?"

"Will you be busy with Janelle tonight?" Travis asked.

Russ heaved a big sigh. "Most likely."

"Great." Travis smiled out the windshield as his brother pulled up to the big building that housed the dogs. "Because Millie is coming over to help me set up a Christmas tree."

Russ snapped his attention to Travis. "You're kidding."

"I am so not," he said. "Our date last night went amazing, and I told her I wanted her help getting the ranch...more festive."

Russ blinked and then laughed. "Festive," he said through chuckles. "Right. No way you used that word."

"Fine, maybe that was Millie's." Travis shrugged, feeling happier than he had in a while.

"You want the ranch to be more festive?"

"Yeah," Travis said. "We love Christmas, and we don't even hang up a wreath."

"*And* you want to see Millie again."

Travis didn't deny or confirm Russ's statement.

"Did you kiss her last night?"

Travis shook his head. "You won't believe this, but her mother was actually waiting on the front steps when we got back."

"Wow." Russ started chuckling again. "You're right, I don't believe that. You sure you didn't just chicken out?"

Travis hadn't chickened out at the wedding, and he was shocked Russ didn't know he'd already kissed Millie. Rex surely knew, and the brothers didn't usually keep secrets from one another.

Russ got out of the truck, and Travis followed him. Several dogs barked as Russ and Travis entered the building, and he stopped at the supply shelf to grab a few leashes. He and Russ would get the dogs outside first so they could clean the kennels, and some of them required leashes.

Travis kept his head down and his hands moving. He had plenty of time to think about Millie and Christmas and the impact all of this would have on the family when he wasn't feet away from some distrusting dogs.

Seth usually kept the bigger and needier dogs away from the ones that had learned and calmed down already. But Seth wasn't here, and Russ and Travis had to do what they could in his absence. And honestly, that meant keeping the dogs alive was their base responsibility.

Travis opened the last gate to let out the last three dogs, and they ran joyfully out into the fenced area Seth called the range. He circled the building and went in a service door several yards down, picked up a shovel and got to work cleaning out their pens.

Russ came around with water, and then loaded up the cart with food. Together, they got the dogs taken care of in an hour and a half, and Travis's back ached.

"You know what would be awesome?" he asked as he rolled the cart back to its spot by the pantry.

"What?"

"Another dog enclosure." Russ looked at Travis, and he knew that glint in his older brother's eye.

"I'm swamped already," he said.

"Then we give more work to Brian, and Tomas, and Darren," he said. "We can afford the overtime."

"Where would we even put the new building?" Travis asked, though he'd already picked out a spot for it. He just needed to talk to Seth, who'd been preoccupied with his wedding, and getting all the new dogs, and planning a honeymoon.

"In the corner," Russ said, naming the exact spot Travis would've chosen. "We extend the fence, what? Twenty feet, and it connects to the existing range. Plan for all the same supply and food storage out there, and done."

"Done," Travis said, wishing it was as easy as waving a wand and saying the word to get the building built. But he knew it would be hours of swinging a hammer and measuring and making things line up.

A new project excited him, though, despite his stony exterior. He couldn't believe he was going to agree to this. Then again, he'd gone out with Millie, and she had much more potential to ruin his life than a new dog enclosure did.

"Okay," he said. "Let's start with the plans this afternoon. We can order supplies tomorrow and get excavating."

Russ whooped, a huge smile crossing his face. "I want to drive the backhoe."

"Of course you do," Travis said. "Fine. Whatever."

Russ clapped him on the shoulder as they walked back to the ranch truck. "And Trav, it's a dog enclosure. We don't need custom cabinets or fancy trim."

"You sure?" Travis gave his brother a smile and climbed into the truck. "Okay, what's next?"

"Horses," Russ said. "With any luck, most of the stalls will be cleaned out by the time we get there."

"Let's hope," Travis said, enjoying a moment in the truck where he could rest.

The necessary work around the ranch got done, as Travis knew it would, and he showered while Russ pulled out blueprint paper. Just the fact that they had blueprint paper in the homestead made Travis realize how awesome the ranch was. He'd designed and built the stables for the horses, both barns, and their personal storage shed. With his skills and mind for design, their ranch really was one of a kind.

After he'd showered, he sat down with Russ and started talking about what kind of enclosure they needed as a back-up.

"I don't see why it has to be lesser than the one we have," Travis said, swiping on his phone. "And we have those plans right here."

"You want to build the exact same thing?"

"No, because the orientation would be wrong. But we need the kennels. The outside doors. The shelving in the pen and the pantry near the front door. We need the outside entrances."

He started to sketch while Russ watched. "How many can we

get in the space we have?" he asked while Travis's pencil went *whoosh whoosh whoosh* across the paper.

Travis glanced down to the part of the paper he hadn't drawn on yet, doing some quick math in his head. "Eight."

"Only eight?"

"Wait, I have an idea." He erased and redrew, pulling the bottom lines longer. "We don't need twenty feet to get to the enclosure if we do it this way."

Russ leaned over, and Travis caught a whiff of manure and horses and sweat. "You better go shower before Janelle shows up," he said, a nice way of saying *you stink.*

If it were Rex talking, he would've just said it, with a "bro" on the end.

Russ got up. "I want to see that when I'm done."

"I'll work fast," Travis said, not even looking up as his brother left. Twenty minutes later, Russ returned to the kitchen counter where Travis had a nearly complete sketch.

He leaned away from it, his fingers tight from where he'd been gripping the pencil. He rolled his shoulders and pushed the drawing toward Russ.

"Sixteen," he said. "We can do them in a double stack, with a door out the front leading to the range. The pens can be left open for a double-long area or closed so dogs can be isolated."

Russ studied the huge sheet of paper, his eyes flitting all over the place. "Entrance on the side. Brilliant." He looked at Travis. "This holds more than the one Seth currently has."

"But not even all the dogs we have right now," Travis said. "And it'll take at least a month to build."

"Let's call Seth." Russ picked up his phone and started tapping on the screen.

"We can't call Seth," Travis said, practically knocking the phone out of his brother's hands. "He said not to call unless something was on fire or one of us was in the hospital."

"We need to get started on this," Russ said.

"Yeah," Travis said. He got up and rounded the counter to

pull a notebook out of the drawer next to the fridge. "And we don't need Seth's permission. He knows we need another building. Let's just start on it. It'll be his Christmas gift."

Travis started making a list of the things they'd need to order and have delivered to the ranch. The only indication that time had passed was the growling of his stomach.

The doorbell rang, and Travis jerked his head up. "What time is it?"

"Five-thirty," Russ said. "Holy cow, Janelle is going to be here soon."

Travis turned toward the front door. "That means that's probably Millie."

A wicked grin graced his brother's face. "I'll get it."

Travis darted in front of him. "No, you will not." He glared Russ right back into the kitchen. "Feed Winner, Cloudy, and Thunder. I'll bring Millie to meet you." He nodded and slicked his palms down the front of his jeans. At least he'd showered before getting too involved in the new project.

Drawing in a deep breath, he reached for the doorknob. He twisted and pulled and Millie stood there, looking radiant and beautiful in a pair of jeans that looked to be painted on her legs, a pink and white checkered shirt that was probably supposed to make her look like a cowgirl, and a pair of sexy cowgirl boots.

Travis lost the ability to speak, let alone think.

"Hey, baby," Millie said easily. "You wanna come help me unload my car?" She hooked her thumb over her shoulder, and Travis jumped into action.

"Unload the car?" he asked, stepping out onto the front porch with her. "What did you bring?"

"Oh, that's a surprise." She gave him a flirty smile that had Travis's brain screaming something about mistletoe as he followed her down the steps.

CHAPTER EIGHT

Millie's first impression of the ranch was of the beauty of the land. The glorious views of the Texas Hill Country couldn't be beat, that was for sure. But this ranch had no personality. The gate had been built decades ago, and none of the brothers had bothered to put any personal touch on it at all.

Millie wasn't a designer, but she did have an eye for details that made a space stand out, feel inviting, and be functional too.

"Holy cow," Travis said as he stood at the back of her car, gazing into the trunk. "I thought we were just doing a Christmas tree?"

"We are, silly." She nudged him a couple of inches to the side so she could lift out the first bin. "Now, start taking stuff in."

"What is all this stuff?"

"Ornaments," she said. "Lights. Garland. A wreath." She started toward the house, tossing over her shoulder, "And we should talk about doing something festive on the front gate."

Travis said something behind her, but she'd already gone too far from him to catch the actual words. She didn't care. She loved setting up decorations, even if there wasn't going to be a party here later.

But there was. Travis just needed to give her more details, and Millie could start planning the most amazing family get-together for the holidays.

She kept them focused on moving in bins and the huge boxed Christmas tree, then she turned to Travis and asked, "So, how many people are we talking for this party?"

He surveyed the piles they'd brought in and took off his cowboy hat. "What?"

"For your family Christmas party," she said. "The brothers, that's five. Parents. Seven. And Jenna. Eight. Will Isaac come? Does he have a girlfriend?" Millie already knew Isaac was dating Luisa Cruise, but she didn't want Travis to know she knew the town gossip. She didn't, not really.

"What about your grandparents?"

"Just my grandmother," he said. "Grandpa died a few years back." He looked at her, and he looked like she'd hit him with a two-by-four. "Grandma will probably come."

"Probably?"

"I haven't exactly talked to anyone about having a party," he said.

Millie's chest tightened. "Oh." She bent to pull the lid off one of the bins. "Okay. So when you do, be sure to let me know. It's hard to plan a party if you don't know the guest list. Or at least a ballpark."

"The ballpark is probably ten people," he said. "Maybe a dozen. I don't see how it would be more than that."

"Well, if Rex was bringing someone. Heck, if all the brothers brought a plus-one, you'd be at ten, and that doesn't include parents, grandparents, or friends."

"A plus-one?"

"Yeah." She giggled and pushed against Travis's chest. "A guest. It's normal to bring a guest to a party."

"Is it now?" He slipped his arms around her waist, and Millie would be lying if she said she hadn't given him the playful nudge to get his arms around her.

"I guess I don't go to a lot of parties," Travis said.

"Oh, cowboy, that's obvious." She laughed and stepped out of his personal space. "Okay, let's start unboxing so you can see your choices."

"I have choices?"

"There's always choices when it comes to decorating," Millie said.

A man cleared his throat, and she looked up to find one of his brothers standing in the doorway.

"Oh," Travis said quickly. "Millie, this is my older brother, Russ. Russ, Millie Hepworth."

"So great to meet you." Millie strode forward and shook his free hand. He held a steaming cup in the other. "I mean, I've probably met you before, but not for a while."

"True," Russ said. "Your brother is Chris, right?"

"One of 'em," she said, smiling. "Are you going to help us with the decorations?"

"No, ma'am." He chuckled. "I'm pretty useless with that stuff." He took a sip of his drink. "But I wanted to let you two know I made hot chocolate if you want some."

Before Millie could answer, a loud crash filled the room. She spun around to find Travis scrambling to stay standing. He grabbed onto the back of the couch, and she saw what had fallen —an end table with a lamp on it.

"I'm okay," Travis said, but Russ just started laughing. The doorbell rang, and Millie felt whipped all over as she turned toward that.

Russ's laughter stopped as if someone had muted his voice, and he hurried back into the kitchen, calling, "Don't you dare answer that!"

Millie giggled and looked at Travis. "Who is it?"

"Janelle Stokes," Travis said. "They're sort of dating? I don't know."

"How can you not know?"

"She broke up with him last week, but—" He cut off as Russ

entered the room again. "Are you guys going to be here? You could help with the tree."

Part of Millie wanted Russ and Janelle to stay and help, and another part really wanted to be alone with Travis. When she pulled out that mistletoe...

"No, we're going to her place, remember?"

"Oh, right," Travis said. "You're showing her the blueprints?"

Russ paused, and Millie noticed the rolled paper in his hand. "Is that okay?"

"It's fine," Travis said, but he wore displeasure in his eyes.

The doorbell rang again, and Russ pulled the door open. "Janelle, hi," he said, stepping outside as he spoke. The door closed a moment later, and Millie watched Travis.

"What's with the blueprints?" she asked. "What are they for?"

"New dog enclosure Russ and I are going to build for Seth." He glanced at the table and bent to right it, setting the lamp back where it went. The shade was askew, and he tried to fix it but only succeeded in ripping it.

"I think I'm done for the night, Mills," he said, and the use of her nickname from a decade ago made everything inside her go soft. "Can I just watch?"

"No," she said with a smile. "You have to choose what you want. But then yes, you can just watch me hang the ornaments if you want."

He sat down on the couch and looked up at her. "Okay, show me the choices."

"All right," Millie said, returning to the bin with the classic red and white ornaments. "But you have to tell me why you don't want Janelle to see your blueprints."

He sighed as she pulled out a box of sparkly, striped ornaments. "We have red and white," she said. "We'll pair this with a metallic. All the color choices get paired with metallics for flowers and lights and all of that."

"I think I know what a metallic is," he said. "Gold or silver, right?"

"Or bronze," she said. "And I've done some copper stuff too, but that was for a bank, and they loved the penny-colored stuff." She beamed a smile in his direction. "Silver would go with red and white, though if you're more of a gold guy, I can make that work too."

Surprise lit his face. "Gold guy?" He laughed, and the atmosphere around them relaxed. "I have no idea what I am."

"Okay," Millie said. "That's another goal of ours tonight, then." She moved over to the next bin. "Here we have a less traditional but still beautiful blue and purple and green assortment." Pulling out a box of ornaments, she handed them to him. "And in this last one, we have a quite formal white and clear."

"Not that one," he said before she even had the bulbs all the way out.

"Colored lights or white?" she asked.

"White," he said.

"We can put colored on the house, if you want," she said. "A neighbor of mine down the street will come and hang them and then take them down. It's a little pricey though."

Travis didn't even flinch, which meant money wasn't a factor in what he decided to do. "Sure," he said. "Sounds great. Colored on the house. I'll call your guy."

"I can arrange it," she said. "You don't need to be home or anything."

"I'm always here," Travis said, a small smile accompanying his words. "Will you come sit for a second? I want to tell you something."

"Oh." Millie stepped past a bin. "Sure." She sat next to Travis, noting the serious expression on his face. She turned toward him and gave him her undivided attention. "What is it?"

"I don't know why I feel like I need to tell you this, but I do. I—my mother is an Alameda."

Millie tried to put the puzzle together with only half the

pieces. The picture felt like it should be there, but it wasn't. "Okay," she said. "The make-up people?"

"Yes, right," he said, exhaling heavily. "A few months ago, she cashed out, and now me and my brothers have a lot of money."

Millie blinked, somehow expecting Travis to suddenly be better than he'd been a few moments ago. But he wasn't. He was still him. Still handsome in that cowboy hat. Still calm in a way Millie really wished she could be. Still steady, and strong, and just...him.

"Okay, so you can afford to pay Mike to come hang your lights." She cocked her head, trying to hear more. "Is that it?"

"Yes," he said. "That's it."

"Okay." She threaded her fingers through his. "Money doesn't really matter to me, Travis."

"Okay," he said. "It's just...some of my other brothers have had some trouble with women once they knew. I'm surprised you hadn't heard. The gossip mill in Chestnut Springs must be rusty or something."

"I don't really care about gossip, either," Millie said.

"Amen to that," He pushed himself off the couch. "Okay, I think I might be able to help without smashing anything."

"What color?" Millie stood too, wishing she'd worn slippers instead of these cowgirl boots. Then she remembered how Travis had looked at them, and she changed her mind again. Though there was something magical about decorating a Christmas tree with a hot cowboy, a cup of hot chocolate, and wearing slippers that Millie really wanted to experience.

But she'd settle for two out of three.

"Blue," Travis said, picking up the box with the blue and purple ornaments in it. "With silver. Yeah?" He looked at her for confirmation, and Millie nodded.

"Silver is in the two bins on the end," she said. "The gray ones."

"Oh, wow," he said. "The bins are color-coordinated. I see it now." He laughed and shook his head. "You're somethin' else, Miss Millie."

"Yeah, well, I'm going to take that as a compliment."

"Good, because it was one." He grinned at her and pushed the red and white bins out of the way, leaving only the blue ones. "Do you want some of that hot chocolate? We might have some popcorn in the cupboard too, and I might be able to pull off making that."

"Absolutely," she said. "Then you can use your muscles to get this tree set up."

"Can't wait," he said, taking her hand and leading her into the kitchen. The space spread out before her, and she liked the huge room that housed the kitchen, eating area, and another, less-formal family room.

"This home is beautiful," she said. "You guys have modernized it well."

"Thanks," he said. "I built these cabinets."

Millie ran her fingers along the top edge of the cabinets in the island while Travis pulled a couple of mugs from one next to the stove. "Wow, they're so beautiful."

"Thanks," he said. "Besides party planning and organizing ornaments in like-colored bins, what do you like to do for fun, Mills?"

"Same and different?" she asked.

He tossed her a look she couldn't quite interpret before he turned to ladle hot chocolate out of the pot on the stove. "Sure."

"Well, I still love to hike," she said. "Remember we did a bit of that when we dated last time?"

He chuckled and kept that cowboy hat concealing his face. When he looked up, he wore delight in a smile on that strong mouth. "I remember you almost killed me on the hike up to Enchantment Rock."

"Oh, please," she said. "*You're* the young, strong cowboy. Not me."

"You said you had enough water, Mills." He advanced toward her, a heated look in those eyes now. "And you so did not."

"We didn't die," she said, taking the mug of hot chocolate he extended toward her and lifting it between them. Wow, he was still fun to flirt with too.

"Different hobby now?" he asked, putting one hand on the counter next to her hip.

Nerves buzzed through her, and she hadn't even broken out the mistletoe yet. She hadn't kissed him the last time they'd dated, and the only kiss they'd shared had been blessed by the magic of a weed. But still. Millie really wanted that zing in her muscles again, the weakness in her back and knees, and everything else that came with kissing a handsome cowboy.

"I think you'll laugh at this one," she said, dropping her gaze to his lips. "But I like to play cards now."

"Cards?"

"Yeah, you know, like bridge and bunko and whatever."

"Like my mother," he said, that smile toying with that mouth.

"I like the older ladies who play, yes," she said. "They're fun, and they don't constantly ask me who I'm dating." She swallowed the rest of the reason she'd stopped hanging out with women her own age, and that was because she'd lost too many boyfriends to supposed best friends.

"Hmm." Travis leaned down and brushed his lips along her cheek. "And what would you tell someone if they asked who you were dating now?"

"I'd say I have this new guy that really makes me smile," she whispered. "And he's so handsome, and I wish he'd take off that cowboy hat and kiss me more often."

Travis pulled in a breath and straightened so he could look right into her eyes. As if in slow motion, he reached up and took off his cowboy hat.

Millie followed his motion, running her fingers through his hair. His eyes drifted closed, and Millie's did too.

"Bro!" A door slammed, and before Millie could register what had happened, Travis was several steps away, a ladle in his hand.

Two men entered the kitchen, one of them saying, "Did you hear the news? Momma and Daddy—oh." He stopped in body and mouth, and she recognized him as the brother who'd told Travis he and Millie were dancing under the mistletoe. "Hello, Millie Hepworth."

A grin curved his lips. "What are you doin' here?"

Not kissing your brother, she thought. *Unfortunately.*

CHAPTER NINE

"She's here to get the homestead lookin' festive," Travis said, nearly knocking the pot with hot chocolate in it on the floor. "What's goin' on with Momma and Daddy?" He cut a look at Millie, wondering what she thought of his crazy family. First Russ acting all weird about Janelle, and now Rex and Griffin showing up out of nowhere. And Seth wasn't even here to complicate things with his bad jokes and kissing Jenna in public.

"They're going to the Dominican Republic next summer," Griffin said, and Travis did drop the ladle into the pot this time.

"What? Dad can't do that."

"They say the doctor cleared him for that clean-water mission they wanted to do."

"That's insane," Travis said. "He can hardly walk." He handed the mug of steaming hot chocolate to Rex, who opened the fridge.

"Do we have any of that canned cream?"

Millie choked, and all three men looked at her. A gorgeous blush moved into her cheeks, and Travis really wished they were alone. "You know, with a hand mixer, you can improve your quality of life," she said.

"Uh, what?" Griffin looked at Travis as if he could translate Woman.

"Do you have a hand mixer?" she asked.

"Yeah." Travis opened a cupboard in the island. "Right there."

"And cream?"

"Rex?"

He pulled it out of the fridge and set it on the counter. Millie got to work plugging in the mixer and pulling a bowl from the same cupboard that the mixer had come from. "You just whip it with a little sugar. It's so much better than that canned stuff."

"Get 'er the sugar, sugar," Griffin teased, and Travis glared at him as he turned to get out the sugar bowl. Millie got the mixer going, and that meant they couldn't talk. She added a few healthy pinches of sugar, and a few minutes later, there was homemade whipped cream on the counter for their hot chocolate.

"Wow," Rex said, spooning some onto his drink. "Thanks, Millie. This is great." He licked his finger and grinned for all he was worth.

And that was Travis's cue to get Millie away from his younger brother. He'd never worried about his brothers stealing his dates as a teenager, because Russ had such different taste in women than him, and Griffin hadn't seemed interested in girls until Travis was finished with school.

But Rex was definitely his biggest competition as an adult, and he didn't need him making eyes at Millie right in front of him. "Should we go decorate the tree?" he asked her, and she scooped a spoonful of cream onto his hot chocolate.

"Yep." She went into the front room, and Travis glared at his brothers.

"Sorry," Griffin said. "We thought you might like some company with Russ gone with Janelle again, bless his heart."

"Yeah," Rex said. "We didn't know you were here with her."

He grinned like a wolf, though, and neither of them seemed keen to get gone.

"Well, I am," he said. "So take your hot chocolate to-go."

Griffin burst out laughing, and Rex just watched him from under the brim of his hat. In that moment, Travis knew exactly what Rex was wondering, because he had the same thoughts in his head—*where's my cowboy hat?*

And why wasn't he wearing it?

He stooped to gather it from where it had fallen on the floor at some point and followed Millie into the living room. She wasn't fluttering around the tree, because he hadn't set it up yet. He gave an exaggerated sigh and sat beside her on the couch, maybe a little too close.

She didn't seem to mind, and he stirred his whipped cream into his hot chocolate. "Sorry about that," he murmured.

"I have brothers," she said. "No apology necessary."

"At your house?" he asked. "Maybe our next date should be there."

"Have you forgotten that I live with my mother?" She giggled and took a sip of her drink. "And is this a date?"

"No," he said. "And yes." He looked at her, glad when their eyes locked. She seemed interested in him, that was for sure. She'd practically *told* him to kiss her, and Travis had been ready to do it—at least until he heard Rex's voice outside. At least his brother's obnoxiously loud voice had finally benefitted Travis. He'd managed to put plenty of distance between him and Millie before Griffin and Rex had come in.

Not that it really mattered. He could kiss who he wanted to. And he and Millie had already locked lips on the dance floor, in front of a lot of people. Surprisingly, no one had said a word to him about it. Maybe they'd been occupied with their own dates and dances. Didn't matter. Travis wasn't going to bring it up, that was for sure.

"What?" Millie asked.

"What what?" Travis echoed.

"You're staring at me."

"Maybe because you're so pretty."

She rolled her eyes though her smile stayed on her face. "Stop it."

"I think I was judging how you took the news that this was our second date."

"Hm." She finished her hot chocolate and set the mug on the end table he'd knocked over earlier. Why he lost control of his body awareness around this woman, he wasn't sure. Something about her simply put his equilibrium off kilter.

"Hm?" he asked.

She snuggled into his side, and he switched hands, holding his hot chocolate in his right only now so he could lift his left arm around her shoulders.

"I kinda thought I was here to work," she said. "You did hire me as your party planner, right?"

"Totally," he said. "But baby, you didn't put those jeans on, with those boots, because you thought you'd be working tonight."

"Trav." She swatted his chest, her mock outrage super cute on her face and in her voice.

"Mills." He pressed a kiss to her temple and whispered, "I *really* like the boots."

She giggled quietly, and they settled into silence, the array of decorations still in front of them. He sipped his hot chocolate, content to let the moment play out for now. Soon enough, Millie straightened, sighed, and said, "All right, cowboy. Break's over. Time to impress me with your Christmas-tree-setting-up skills."

"Oh, you're in for a disappointment." He put his mug on the opposite end table and stood up. "But I'll try." He pulled his pocketknife out of his pocket and sliced open the box that held the artificial tree. He hated how the branches felt against his skin, but he got the widest part into the tree stand with relative ease. The other sections went right on top, and Millie plugged them all into each other, and then into the wall.

The tree lit up with brilliant white lights, and Travis marveled at it. "How did you know I'd say white lights?" he asked.

"Not sure," she said, and she was so angelic in the light from the tree. "But I'm glad I guessed right." She handed him a box of blue and purple ornaments. "It's your turn for the same-different game."

"Mm hm. What was the topic?"

"Something you like to do." She began to hang ornaments on the tree, and Travis joined her, the warmth from her body making him feel woozy. Or maybe that was the rich hot chocolate Russ was famous for.

"Bro," Rex said from the doorway, and Travis turned toward him. "We're heading back to town."

"Okay," Travis said. "Good to see you guys."

"We'll be out in the morning to help with the chores."

"Yeah." Travis turned back and hung a blue ball on a limb. "Oh, wait. Did Russ text you about the new dog enclosure?"

"No." Rex took a step into the room, allowing space for Griffin to join them. "What's that about?"

"We're ordering the supplies tomorrow," he said. "Christmas present for Seth. It would be awesome to have you guys help."

"Of course."

"Brian, Tomas, and Darren are going to pick up the slack around the ranch." At least Travis hoped they were. Russ had said he'd text everyone.

"Perfect." Rex nodded, and the two of them turned to leave.

Travis waited until he heard the back door close, and then he took a deep breath. "Let's see. Something I still really like is building things with my hands."

"And something new I don't know about?"

He searched for something new and exciting about himself. "I dunno, Mills. I'm about the same."

"Come on," she said. "That's not true at all."

"No?"

She shook her head, her eyes gleaming. But she didn't offer him any suggestions, and Travis knew she wouldn't give up either. "Uh, I like sour candy."

"Uh, lame," Millie said. "I could've said I like peanut butter cups, but I told you something real."

"Something real," he muttered as he moved around the tree, adding another ornament in a bare spot. "I'd like to play the guitar better than I currently do."

"We're getting there now," she said. "You should take a lesson."

"I don't have time for lessons."

"Sure you do," she said, joining him in the narrow space between the tree and the wall. "And bonus, you could get off the ranch and come see me in town after the lesson."

Travis glanced at her. "Do you have a neighbor who does lessons?"

"As a matter of fact..." She laughed, and Travis hooked another bulb over a limb.

"Wow, you know everyone," he said.

"I've been back in town for a couple of months," she said. "I literally don't know anyone."

"You know me."

"Well, that's true." She pressed in close to him and stretched up to place a kiss on his cheek. "And you're all that matters." She slipped away from him then, and Travis wondered what good deed he'd done to get this woman in his life.

His head spun a little bit, because the speed at which their relationship had taken off would make anyone a little light-headed. He needed to know when he could see her again, but tomorrow night was dinner at his parents' house. Even Seth had come while he was dating Jenna, but Travis told himself that Jenna worked in the evenings and couldn't have come anyway.

Millie could.

The real question was: Did Travis want her to?

Millie appeared at the edge of the tree again, something

silver and glinting in her arms. "These are called picks. You just stick them straight into the branches." She plucked one from the pile and did so. "Anywhere that needs filling."

"Are they flowers?"

"Silver poinsettias," she said. "And some holly berries. They're pretty, right?" She gave him an armful and took his empty ornament box. "I didn't get a tree skirt, because I wasn't sure what you had or what color scheme you would choose. But I can do that tomorrow and come back."

"I have dinner at my parents' tomorrow," Travis said, his mouth suddenly dry. Why was asking her out so dang hard? They'd *kissed* already, for crying out loud. But wow, the thought of doing it again had his palms sweating and his heart scampering around his chest. What if the first time was a fluke and he crashed and burned the second time?

"What about lunch?" he asked. "Or you can come out whenever is convenient for you, and we can just...talk."

"I can bring you lunch," she said.

"I'll pay for it," he said.

"What time do you normally break for lunch?"

"Whenever," he said. "There's no real normal. When a chore gets done and we're hungry, we come in and eat."

"All of you?"

"Yeah, usually," he said. "And Brian and Tomas and Darren."

"So seven men." Millie's eyebrows went up.

"We can take a walk around the ranch," he said. "We have a couple of pretty amazing bridges that go over the river."

"Trying to get me alone, Mister?"

"Oh, yeah," he said, matching her tease for tease. "Was that part not obvious?"

She laughed, and Travis relaxed. This was Millie. He'd already kissed her, and he hadn't forgotten how, despite his long hiatus from women.

"I'll order pizza," he said. "If you'll pick it up, we'll be golden."

"Someone has metallics on the brain," she said with a smile. They finished decorating the tree, and Millie scooted it right in front of the window. Travis helped her take all the bins back out to her car, and he broke down the box the Christmas tree had come in, sticking it in their recycling bin.

She loitered by her car, playing with her keys. Travis knew this tactic, and she didn't want to leave without saying good-bye. He didn't want her to either, and he approached slowly, trying to calm down.

They hadn't danced, and she hadn't brought any mistletoe. At least the noxious weed hadn't made an appearance.

Yet, he thought.

He felt like he was on an emotional roller coaster with this woman. Nervous one moment and then relaxed the next. He gestured toward the window, where the tree twinkled merrily. "Thank you for this. What do I owe you?"

"I'll figure it out with the supplies and everything and bill you. Okay?"

"Sure."

"Do you use pay-to?"

"Pay-what?"

She smiled and shook her head, wrapping her arms around the back of his neck. "It's an app, Trav. You really should download it and hook your bank account to it. Then you can spend some of your money."

Travis pulled in a breath, quickly realizing Millie was teasing him about the app and not that he was rich. "I bought a new truck."

"I figured."

"And then you can pay me for the pizza with a couple of taps and for tonight and the party and all of that."

"All of that? There's more?"

"I hope so," she whispered, tipping up onto her toes. Before Travis could seal their amazing night with a kiss, headlights cut across him and Millie as Russ pulled into the driveway.

"Foiled again," Millie said, stepping out of his arms and opening her car door. "Maybe tomorrow, cowboy." With that, she got behind the wheel and started her car. She rolled down her window and added, "And you still owe me a dance."

He leaned his elbows against the roof of her car, peering inside at her. "Yeah, well, you didn't bring any mistletoe."

"Next time," Millie said and flipped the car into reverse.

Travis waved as she backed out, but her headlights kept him from seeing anything she might have done.

"I'm sorry," Russ said, coming out of the garage. "What rotten timing."

"It's fine," Travis said. "Wasn't in the stars tonight." But tomorrow...Travis was going to kiss Millie no matter what the stars or the cards or anyone else said.

CHAPTER TEN

"Events by Millie," Millie hated answering her phone that way, but she'd paid a fee on her cell phone to get a second number specifically for her business. Since all of her creativity went into the party planning, she'd had nothing left to give the name of her business.

"Yes, hello Millie, dear. It's Diana Toolson."

"Oh, hello, Mrs. Toolson." Millie looked away from the laptop in her bedroom, because someone as proper and stuffy as Diana Toolson required all of her brain power. Then she wouldn't say something sarcastic or anything that the older woman could deem as inappropriate.

"How can I help you?" she asked, hoping the woman had a major event on the horizon.

"I heard you were back in town and doing events," she said.

"Both true." Millie leaned back in her chair.

"How's your momma?"

Millie sincerely hoped this was not a social call. "She's doing okay, ma'am."

"Good," Diana said. "Good. Listen, I'm calling because I'd like to renew my vows in a small, private ceremony, and I thought you'd be just the person to help."

"Of course," Millie said, reaching for her laptop and clicking quickly to get to a new client page. "Tell me everything you're thinking."

"We got engaged fifty years ago at Chestnut Springs," she said. "I'd love to have the vows renewed there, on January twentieth."

The hike to Chestnut Springs wasn't terrible, but the weather could be in January. "Okay," Millie said, her memory tickling with something. What, she couldn't quite remember at the moment. "How many people? They can hike up there in dress clothes? Shoes? Heels?"

"Oh, it doesn't need to be fancy, dear," she said. "Just me and Brent, and our two daughters. Their husbands. Maybe the grandkids..."

"How many people is that?" Millie asked, her fingers hovering above the keyboard.

"Probably twenty," Diana said, and Millie wondered how many grandchildren the woman had.

"Twenty," she repeated. "Okay. Are you looking for a meal up there? Something at your home afterward?"

"Something up there," she said. "We'd want the place to ourselves, naturally."

"Oh." Millie sat back from her computer again. "Well, Mrs. Toolson, Chestnut Springs is a public place. I'm not sure you can rent it and close the trail and springs to everyone else."

"That's why I called you, dear," she said, and Millie knew then that she'd fail Mrs. Toolson. "We had ham sandwiches on our first hike there, and I've already got the best caterer lined up. Shall I pass on his name?"

"Uh, yes?" Millie wasn't sure why she'd phrased it as a question, only that it had come out that way. She usually did the whole event, and the person who'd hired her didn't know who to get for catering or music or décor. With the vow renewal being at the springs, there would be very little décor. Music would be hard, but Millie had done remote events before, and she had some killer Bluetooth speakers.

But it seemed like all Diana Toolson needed was someone to reserve the springs—something Millie was fairly certain she couldn't do anyway.

"So what do you think?" Diana asked, and Millie realized she'd zoned out. "What would your fee be?"

The fact that she called it a fee also annoyed Millie. "You know what?" she asked. "I'm going to need to do a little investigative work to see if it's even possible to reserve Chestnut Springs for a private event. If that's the case, I'll let you know how much this event will cost. Sound good?"

"Yes," Diana said. "I look forward to hearing from you." The call ended, and Millie stared at her phone in disgust. Then she dialed the city offices and got transferred to the parks department. If there was one good thing—besides Travis Johnson—about being back in Chestnut Springs, it was that she knew exactly who to call to get the answers she needed.

"Hey, Ramon," she said, going on to explain the situation in as few words as possible. Travis would be so proud.

"Yeah, I don't think so, Millie," Ramon said. "I mean, you're welcome to set up there. But we can't close the entire trail for a private event."

"But why?" she asked, just so she'd have something to report to Diana. "We close the pool for private events all the time, and the city owns and operates that."

"I—we—good point."

"Can you find out?" Millie asked. She wasn't terribly keen on doing the event at the springs in the middle of winter, but a job was a job. And Millie couldn't afford to be too picky, though she did have more breathing room since landing the contract job with Serendipity.

"I'll find out," Ramon said. "Give me a couple of days. We actually have our monthly meeting on Monday night."

"I'll hear from you after that, then," she said.

"Have a blessed day," Ramon said, and Millie smiled. She'd forgotten the Southern drawl of people who said that, and she sure did like it.

Her mother knocked on her door, and Millie got up. "Hey, Momma." She gave her mom a quick hug. "I'll heat up leftovers for you, okay? I'm late to pick up the pizza and head out to the ranch."

"Actually," her mother said, and Millie saw her romantic walk with Travis on some pretty Texas bridges fade right before her eyes. "I was wondering if I might come. I'll stay out of the way, and we could take our walk out there." Her mother's eyes held so much pleading and hope that Millie couldn't just dismiss her.

"I haven't left town in so long," she added, and Millie couldn't say no.

"Let me call Travis, okay?"

Her mom nodded and shuffled down the hall, already dressed with her sneakers on and everything. Millie didn't call, but she tapped out a quick text.

I need a raincheck on that kiss. My mother is coming with me.

She wasn't desperate to kiss Travis; it only felt like it. She told herself there was plenty of time, and she should probably know him a little bit better anyway. Just because he made her feel more alive than any man had in years didn't mean she needed to kiss him the moment she met him.

Sorry, she added when Travis didn't respond right away. She slipped into her cowgirl boots again, because Travis sure had seemed to like those. At the last minute, she decided to change her shoes. If she and her mother were going to walk a mile, she didn't want it to be in the boots.

Finally ready, she joined her mom in the living room. "Ready?"

"I'm coming?"

"Yep." Millie steadied her mother as she stood, and they went out the front door and down the steps at a slow, agonizing pace. "We have to stop and get the pizza, and then we'll be on our way."

Her mother was having a good day, at least. Millie reasoned that her mother was an amazing woman, and no one would care that she was there.

Except her.

She pulled up to The Flying Dog to pick up the pizza, noticing that she'd received a text on the way over. *No problem*, Travis had said. *Favorite soda flavor?*

Grape, she tapped out as she ran inside and gave the kid there her name. *Yours?*

A minute and five pizzas later, she was back in the car, ready to make the quick fifteen-minute trip to Chestnut Ranch.

Her phone beeped, and she managed to catch the previous of Travis's text before it disappeared off her screen.

Gross. Mine's root beer.

Millie smiled, because she loathed root beer with everything inside her. She and Travis didn't seem to have a lot in common, but they sure did get along just fine. More than fine, as Millie didn't want to get to know anyone but him.

Of course, you felt that way about Shane too, she told herself. And look at what happened with him.

So maybe more time to get to know Travis was a good idea. She didn't need to give away her heart if the man she gave it to wasn't willing to keep it safe.

She made the turn onto the ranch road, and drove past the beautiful Wright estate. The gate for Chestnut Ranch came into view, and Millie's excitement grew. "All right, Momma," she said. "We're here."

"This is lovely," her mother said. "Now, how are you goin' to introduce this man of yours?"

"Mom, you've met him already—twice."

"Yes, but no one introduced him. Is he your boyfriend?"

Millie thought about the conversation they'd had last night, right in that very living room. "Yes," she said. "Happy now?"

"Very," her mother said with sparkling eyes.

Millie got out of the car and opened the back door. Before she could heft the pizzas into her arms, Travis called, "I'm comin', Mills. Let me get them."

She'd let him all right, because then he'd put those muscles on display again. Turning, she almost ran into him as he jogged toward her.

"Hi," she said, enjoying the long-sleeved denim shirt that kept his skin clean and safe. The beard was just so sexy, and that smile... She was shocked no one in Chestnut Springs had snatched him right up.

"Hi." He swept a quick kiss along her cheek, the touch of his lips there and gone before she even registered it. He bent into the car while Russ appeared to help her mother inside. Millie was impressed by these Johnsons, as their mother sure had raised them right.

"Five pizzas for eight people," he said as he straightened. "Feels a little ridiculous, doesn't it?"

"And a salad," she said, reaching for the garden salad she'd gotten for herself. "I can pay for that."

"Nope," he said. "Just tell me how much. I downloaded that app and everything."

"Wow, look at you, Mister Johnson."

"Hey, this dog can learn new tricks," he said with a chuckle. They walked up the front sidewalk together, and as they climbed the steps, he asked, "So how much?"

"Uh, seventy-six dollars," she said. "And some change. Seventy-six is fine." She darted in front of him and opened the door so he could walk through unhindered. The scent of coffee and cologne met her nose, and she actually liked it. She stayed behind to close the door, and when she made it to the kitchen, she was the last one to arrive.

The Johnson brothers were treating her mother like a queen, with Griffin handing her a glass of iced tea and Russ leading the three dogs over to her as if she were made of glass. Her mother loved dogs, so Russ had just secured his spot right inside Momma's heart.

"Pizza," Travis said, setting the boxes on the counter, and a couple of the men whooped. Millie guessed that they didn't host big lunches at the homestead very often, and she wondered if that was a tradition Travis wanted.

A type of organized chaos followed, and Millie liked watching the men pass out plates and reach over one another for the pizza they wanted.

"What do you want, baby?" Travis asked, staying out of the way of the fray.

"Nothing with fruit or veggies."

"Really?" His arm slipped behind her back, and Millie leaned into him, basking in the warmth and comfort of his presence. "That surprises me."

"With pizza, it's all about the meat and cheese," she said. "Though there's this spot in San Antonio that has the greatest Caprese pizza, and that has green stuff *and* tomatoes."

"Yeah, I draw the line at salad on pizza," he said.

Millie was sure he didn't quite know what Caprese actually was, but she just smiled and snuggled into him. When the brothers and their ranch hands headed over to the table, Travis stepped over to the counter and picked up a plate. He put a couple of slices of pizza on it for her and handed it to Millie.

"They left you a spot." He nodded toward the table, which only had one chair left.

"Where will you sit?"

"Wherever." He picked up another plate and loaded it with pizza. "We could go outside."

"Alone," she whispered, and Travis's eyes locked onto hers. Millie lifted her eyebrows and added, "I'm making a break for it. Momma's occupied for at least a few minutes."

And maybe she'd get her kiss after all.

CHAPTER ELEVEN

Travis ate with Millie on the back patio, in clear eyesight of everyone eating at the table. They seemed to be laughing and having a good time, and this lunch was quite a bit different than the cowboys making quick sandwiches or heating up whatever Russ or Seth had made for dinner the night before. Sometimes they had something Momma had sent home with them in neat, plastic containers.

He liked the new energy at the homestead, and he wondered why they'd always kept such a boundary between them and the ranch hands they employed. Russ was the one with a degree in ranch management, but as far as Travis could tell, he simply did what their father had done.

Which was fine. Travis wasn't going to rock the boat. He did feel a great responsibility to have something to say to Millie, but his mind whirred, never settling on any one thing. She didn't say anything either, and they'd had silences between them before. But this one felt charged, awkward, especially with Rex's booming voice coming through the closed patio doors.

"Quiet today," Millie said, and humiliation rushed through Travis.

"Nothin' to say," he said. "Anything exciting happen for you this morning?"

"Oh, I was finalizing a few things on my website," she said. "And then Diana Toolson called."

"Oh boy," Travis said. "The Toolson's. Not sure that's going to be exciting."

"Hey," she said, but she started giggling too.

Travis finished his pizza and stood up to collect their plates. "Do you think we could sneak away for a quick walk?" He glanced toward the party happening inside.

"I told Momma I'd walk with her too," Millie said. "But we could go for a few minutes, if your brothers can handle her."

Travis went through the glass doors to a rowdy round of laughter. No one noticed him as he crossed to the trashcan, and he had to touch Russ's shoulder to get his brother's attention. "I'll be back in a few," he said. "You guys okay here?"

"Yeah, sure." And then Russ was back to the conversation, something about Tomas's date with Lucy and the dancing that had ensued.

Travis felt like a fraud, and he escaped the kitchen as quickly as he could. Millie had waited for him outside, and Travis took her hand as they started walking.

"You're squeezing tight," Millie said, and Travis released her as quickly as he'd slipped his fingers through hers.

"Sorry."

"What's wrong?" she asked.

Travis didn't need to reveal all of his flaws right now. It had been less than a week since the dance at the wedding, but Travis had never needed too terribly long to know how he felt about a woman.

But she needs some time, he told himself. He didn't need to repeat his mistakes and break-ups of the past.

"Trav?" Millie stepped in front of him, blocking his retreat from everyone that was more fun than him.

"Look," he said. "I'm not mad or anything. But I'm not Rex,

or Griffin, or even Russ. I'm quiet sometimes, and well, that's how it is." He drew in a deep breath, but he felt like he'd just gotten off the treadmill.

"I know that," Millie said.

"I'm not the fun Johnson brother," he said. "Maybe you'd be happier with Griffin. He's close to your age, and he's a lot more lively than me." He stepped around her, his strides lengthening.

"Travis," Millie said from behind him. "Wait."

He stopped suddenly, and she ran past him. Turning back, she tucked her hair and sucked in a breath. She looked concerned, her blue eyes wide as she searched his face.

"It's fine," he said. "Sorry that was…I'm a little sensitive about being the boring brother."

"You're not the boring brother."

"Rex has actually called me that before."

"And look who has the girlfriend," Millie said, smiling.

But Travis couldn't return it. "I know you didn't mean anything when you said I was being quiet today. I know that. Let's just forget it."

"No," Millie said quickly. "I'm not going to forget it." She backed up a step, but she didn't look away from him. "I apologize that I said you were quiet. Quiet doesn't bother me."

"Millie, I really don't want to talk about this."

"I don't want to go out with Griffin," she said, lifting her chin. "I like *you*, Travis, whether you're talking or not talking or whatever."

Travis felt like someone had injected a storm into his bloodstream. "I'm sorry," he said. "I just…"

"You should never be sorry for telling me how you feel." Millie reached up and cradled his face in her hand. "Okay? I don't care if you only say two words, as long as I know how you feel."

"I feel like a fool," he whispered. All the fight inside him faded to nothing, and he hung his head, causing her to drop her hand.

"Travis, we get to be ourselves with each other."

He looked at her, pure hope filing him over and over again. Could that really be true? Could he just be himself with this woman? He'd never been able to do that, and all of his past relationships had failed, because he'd never been enough for the women he'd dated. Even the one he'd somehow managed to hide his true self from long enough to get a ring on her finger had figured it out eventually.

Millie wrapped her arms around him and held on, and Travis hugged her back. "Thanks," he whispered.

"Even the big, strong cowboy has a soft side," she said. "I like that, Trav. Very sexy."

"Yeah?" He'd never considered his weakness to be something anyone would like.

"Yeah." She pulled back and gazed up at him. "And don't look now, but my momma is coming this way, and I'm going to need to go help her on the uneven grass."

Travis twisted, and Millie stepped out of his arms. "Yeah, go." He went with her, pressed a kiss to her forehead and added, "I have to get back to work anyway. I'll call you after dinner with my folks?"

"Can't wait," Millie said, and Travis couldn't help the slip of foolishness still moving through him. He couldn't believe he'd told Millie that she should go out with Griffin, especially when his younger brother spilled from the homestead with a slice of pizza stuck to the top of his head.

TRAVIS DIDN'T SAY MUCH DURING DINNER AT HIS MOTHER'S, which wasn't that unusual. He knew his brothers hadn't meant to exclude him. In fact, he was sure they'd embraced Millie's momma so he'd have the opportunity to be alone with Millie.

His mother made a beautiful cheeseburger with homemade French fries, and he would've wrestled anyone for the sweet potato fries with chipotle seasoning. Everyone loved them, and his mom was smart—she made a ton of them.

"You've been quiet tonight, dear," his momma said as Griffin got up to get coffee mugs.

"Yeah," Travis said. "Not much to say."

"What's new at the ranch?"

Travis inhaled and pushed out a breath. "Everything." He gave his mom a quick smile. "Seth bein' gone is hard."

"I'll bet."

"Russ and I are going to build him another dog enclosure for Christmas."

She accepted the cup of coffee from Griffin, smiling at him fondly. "Thank you, baby," she said before focusing on Travis again. "A new dog enclosure. That's ambitious."

"Probably, yeah," he said. "But we can do it."

Momma glanced toward Daddy, and Travis followed her gaze. "Daddy will want to come help," she said, hiding her mouth behind her mug. "Don't you dare let him."

"How's he going to deal with things in the Dominican Republic?" Travis asked.

"He'll use a walker," she said. "And a wheelchair. It was the only way I'd agree to go with him." She lit up as she started talking about their upcoming service mission, though it was still months and months away.

"What do you want for Christmas dinner?" she asked, changing the topic quickly.

"What I always want for dinner," he said, kicking a smile at her.

"We can't have steak for Christmas."

"Why not?"

She shook her head. "I'll do steak bites for the party."

"Party?" His heart leapt to the back of his throat, and he stared at his mother.

"Yes," she drawled. "We always have a little get-together a

few weeks into December. We'll wait until Seth and Jenna get
home, of course, and—"

"Momma," Travis interrupted, needing to get the words out
before they choked him. "I want to have the party at the homestead. On the ranch."

Griffin set a cup of coffee down in front of him, clearly
lingering to listen to the conversation. In fact, everyone had
stopped talking and was now watching Travis. He glanced down
the table to Russ and Rex, who both sat there silently.

His mother made a noise sort of like a bike tire leaking. "At
the ranch?"

"We have no traditions there, Momma," he said. "And we
need some."

"And his girlfriend is a party planner," Rex said.

"Shut up," Travis hissed to his youngest brother. But the
dreaded word had been said.

"Girlfriend?" His mother's interest would be the death of
Travis. And a slow one.

Travis swung his attention back to his momma. "It's new,
Momma," he said. "No big deal, but yes, I did ask her to plan us
a party out at the ranch. You guys can come out there." He
threw a look at his father that he hoped would operate as an
SOS. His mother often said she was the one who was outnum-
bered, but she didn't realize her opinion counted as ten votes.
She could sway the whole family with a single look.

"Sally," Daddy said, drawing out her name into four syllables.
"Let the boys host this year. Less work for you." He took a sip of
his coffee, his piece said.

Thanks, Daddy, Travis thought, sending him a quick smile. He
looked at his mother, his eyebrows raised.

"Can your girlfriend make sure we have steak at the party?"

Travis chuckled and ducked his head. "I'm sure she can."

"Who is this woman?"

"Momma, I don't want to be grilled," he said.

"Come on," she said. "I can't know her name?"

Travis sighed just to prolong the moment. He wasn't really going to withhold Millie's identity from his mother. "Millie Hepworth," he said.

"Yeah," Rex said. "The woman he danced with at the wedding last week?" He grinned like a wolf, and Travis wanted to sock him in that mouth that never stopped.

"I didn't see him dance with anyone," Momma said.

"Oh, I did," Rex said.

"Rex," Travis growled, getting up from the table. "Thanks for dinner, Momma." He leaned down and hugged her tight. "Love you."

"Love you too, baby. You're going already?"

Russ was up too, and Travis suddenly couldn't wait to leave. "Yep."

"We have so much to do on the ranch, Momma," Russ added, and they headed out. Once in the safety of the truck, Travis glanced at Russ.

"Do you think I'm too quiet?"

Russ watched him, and Travis didn't like it. He wished he hadn't said anything. "Of course not," Russ said. "And even if I did, why would it matter? You're who you are, and if you don't want to talk all the time, who cares?"

Travis nodded, unsure why he needed so much reassurance about this. "I mean, Rex always has something to say."

"Do you seriously want to be like Rex?" Russ shook his head and chuckled darkly. "Don't get me wrong, *bro*. I love him, because he's my brother. But his voice grates on my nerves sometimes."

"Maybe he's just one extreme, and I'm the other," Travis said.

"I prefer your extreme," Russ said. "Honestly."

"Okay." Travis didn't need more than that. "Do you want to tell me about Janelle?"

"Not yet," Russ said, looking out his window, his voice fading at the end.

"Fair enough. I can't believe I forgot Momma did a party for Christmas."

"Well, she didn't do it last year," Russ said. "And the year before that, Daddy had just fallen."

Travis nodded, glad it had been a few years since she'd done a party.

"Do you want to talk about Millie?" Russ asked.

"Not yet," Travis said, because he thought he should probably kiss her without the addition of mistletoe before he said anything to anyone.

CHAPTER TWELVE

Millie's breath came quickly as she continued to climb, her blonde ponytail swaying with every step. "Holy sweet tea," Angela Brunner said behind her. "I don't remember...this trail...being so...dang hard."

Millie couldn't answer, because she was breathing too hard. The scenery surrounding Chestnut Springs always made her feel small and insignificant among all of God's beauty. At the same time, the miles of rolling hills and trees and fields made her feel strong and powerful and full of joy.

She loved using her muscles, though right now, her right calf was screaming at her to *stop. Stop already!*

She reached the top of the trail and stopped, Ang wheezing as she joined her. Their eyes met, and Millie grinned through her sweat and heavy breathing. "I'm dying," she said, reaching for the straw connected to her water backpack.

"We haven't done this one for too long," Ang said. "We should do it every Friday for a while."

"Are you kidding?" Millie laughed, but the sound was more like a strangled gasp. She stretched her calf, but the pain remained. They hiked together every Friday morning, and Millie was glad for the change in her exercise routine. Plus, she loved seeing Ang, who worked as an aesthetician and could set her own schedule.

"We have to do something easy next week," Millie said, lifting up on her toes to further work out her muscle. "Though the view up here is fantastic." She gazed out over the countryside from the top of Mount Ol' Baldy, and she wondered where Travis had lived in nearby Concan.

"Really rejuvenates the soul, doesn't it?" Ang asked.

"It really does." Millie drew in a long breath and stretched her arms above her head, moving through a standing yoga routine that would bring her heart rate down.

"I got your website," Ang said.

"Yeah?" Millie glanced at her as she walked further along the rock. "How did it look?"

"It's adorable, of course." Ang threw her a smile over her shoulder. "I'd hire you."

"Thanks." Millie couldn't help smiling. "I designed it myself."

"It's amazing," she said. "In fact, I'm hoping you'll be available for a surprise party for Jack."

"Sure," she said, following her friend and still taking in the spectacular scenery in the Texas Hill Country. "His birthday is in March, right?"

"Yep, the fourth."

Millie stretched her back. "Right. March fourth. I remember. How old will he be?"

"The big four-oh," Ang said. "Which is why we need an epic party. I mean, *epic*." Her blue eyes sparkled like sapphires, and Millie liked that her husband made her so happy. They had two cute boys together too, and while Angela was a few years older than her, Millie sure did like spending time with her.

"Epic takes time to plan," she said. "I'll put you on my calendar when I get home."

"Thanks, Mills. What else is new with you?"

Millie sighed, toying with the idea of telling Ang about

Travis. They weren't in a secret relationship, and frankly, Millie was surprised her mother hadn't spread the word far and wide.

"I'm sort of seeing someone new," she said.

"Millie." Ang darted over to her. "Sort of? Someone new? I thought we weren't dating for a while after Mitch?"

"Is that what I said?"

"Yes," Ang said with too much force. "That is what you said."

"Well, this guy asked me to dance at a wedding, and I couldn't say no."

"Yes, you can," Ang said. "You just say it. No. No, thank you. Sorry, dude." Her Texan accent sure was cute when she got animated.

"It was Travis Johnson." Millie watched Angela's whole demeanor change in the blink of an eye.

"Oh, well, that changes things."

Millie had never been the type to kiss and tell, and she kept their mistletoe kiss under her tongue. "Does it? In what way?"

"I heard that his momma sold some huge part of some company, and they have a ton of money."

Millie had heard the same thing—from the horse's mouth. "And that means I can date him? Because he's rich?"

"Well, no," Ang said. "But money doesn't hurt, you know?"

"Doesn't it?" Millie wasn't so sure about that. She knew plenty of men with a lot of money who didn't know how to treat a lady, and Travis definitely did.

"We're not going to argue about money again," Ang said, smiling as she shook her head. She rolled out her shoulders and reached up to pull her own blonde ponytail tighter. "And Travis. He's quite the catch, isn't he?"

"Is he?" Millie asked. "Why do you think that?"

"Well, number one, all those Johnson boys are kind of mysterious, and none more than Travis. He doesn't come to town much, and even when he does, there's not a lot to say about him."

Millie had plenty to say, but she once again held it back. Her feelings for him were growing steadily every time she saw him, and she rather liked unraveling the mystery around the cowboy billionaire.

"Plus, he's hot," Ang said with a giggle. "Don't tell Jack I said that."

"Yeah, because I talk to Jack all the time," Millie said, rolling her eyes. "Now, come on. We have to get back. I have to pick up a tree skirt and go out to the ranch today."

"Ooh, seeing your cowboy boyfriend again?"

"I'm planning a Christmas party for his family," Millie said, making their relationship sound more professional than it actually was.

"Ooh, ritzy," Ang said. "Should we run down?"

Millie moaned, but she nodded. "But it's not a race."

"Oh, yes, it is," Ang said, already moving toward the trail they'd come up. She'd win for sure, because her legs were twice as long as Millie's.

With one last regular breath, Millie started jogging, her eyes trained on the ground. The last thing she needed was a sprain or a break. Then she'd never make it to the ranch to see the hot, mysterious Travis Johnson.

A FEW HOURS LATER, SHE PULLED INTO THE DRIVEWAY AT Chestnut Ranch, armed with the tree skirt and a plan to get a date for that night. Travis had not asked her out for that Friday night, but she wasn't leaving without him or a good reason he couldn't take her to dinner.

Heck, she'd take him to dinner if that was what it took.

Millie was surprised by the strength of her feelings, but there they were, pulsing and vibrating inside her.

She wasn't sure where Travis was, as she'd texted him to say she was on her way out to finish the tree, and he hadn't responded. He could be anywhere on the ranch, and she didn't even know how big it was.

Ringing the doorbell didn't bring anyone to greet her, and Millie hesitated. Could she simply try the door? All she needed to do was spread the tree skirt on the floor, and the tree would be done. It was a thirty-second job she was hoping to turn into an afternoon with her cowboy.

Ridiculous, she thought, the faint sound of hammering coming from behind her. "Ah-ha," she murmured to herself. Travis had told her he was going to build a dog enclosure for his brother, but she hadn't realized they'd be starting the very next day.

Weren't there holes to dig and foundations to pour? Millie admittedly didn't know everything about construction, but she knew that much.

She soon realized that distances on the ranch were very much like they were in Vegas—much farther away than they looked. When she reached the huge fenced area where dogs were romping around, she definitely saw two men working a little further out.

She was really regretting her hike to the summit of Mount Baldy that morning by the time she'd tromped through the long grass to the spot where Russ and Travis were working. Russ saw her first, and he lifted his hand in greeting, nodding to Travis in the next moment.

He turned toward her, and Millie almost fell down. The sight of that sexy cowboy hat, those broad shoulders and that tool belt slung dangerously low around his waist... It felt like air was the wrong thing to breathe.

Travis came toward her, and she lifted the tree skirt, which she'd ridiculously brought with her. "I came to finish the decorating."

"Hey, baby," he said, leaning down and kissing her cheek. "You could've just gone in. I can't remember the last time we locked anything at the homestead."

Millie thought about the walk back and glanced at the pickup truck parked nearby. She was going back in that thing, that was for sure. She looked up at Travis, and he seemed puzzled for a moment.

"You're building without a foundation?"

"Oh, uh." He spun back to where he and Russ had a ton of lumber and were obviously building walls. "Yeah, it's construction in stages," he said. "We can frame all the walls and then attach them to the cement foundation once that's ready. It'll keep things moving forward, and things will go fast once the foundation is cured."

"Fascinating."

He looked back at her, that heat that had always been between them sparking in his eyes.

"Maybe you could take a break?" she asked. "I know you're super busy and all of that. More work than men, but...I was hoping to see those bridges you told me about."

And get a date for that night, but Millie was willing to bide her time. "Plus, there's no way I can walk all the way back to the homestead. So I need a ride at the very least."

Travis laced his fingers through hers and squeezed. "You can't walk back to the homestead?"

"I hiked Old Baldy this morning," she said.

"Wow," he said. "That's out near where I used to live."

"I know," she said. "I thought about you when I was on the summit." She gave him what she hoped was a coy smile.

"Can you walk to the bridge? It's just over there." He didn't look toward anything or point to anything. He seemed to only be able to look at her, and Millie wished his brother were anywhere but here with them.

"I think I can handle getting to the bridge," she said.

"All right." He turned back to Russ and let go of her hand. "I'm gonna take a break, Russ. You okay here?"

"Yep," his brother called. "Go. Have fun."

Travis took off his tool belt, and Millie actually mourned the loss of it. If there was anything better than a cowboy for her, it was a carpenter cowboy.

He set his tools in the back of the truck almost lovingly, and then he took the tree skirt from her. "This is nice, Mills." He held it out in front of him as he examined it. "Did you make it?"

She laughed and shook her head. "No way," she said. "I don't sew. Me and needles don't get along. I found it at Heatherford's."

"My momma loves Heatherford's," Travis said, turning to place the tree skirt on the back seat of the truck. "So that should win her over for sure."

Surprise darted through Millie. "Do I need to win her over?"

Travis returned to her and took her hand in his again. "I mean, maybe? She was surprised I wanted to do a party out here."

Now a pair of hands squeezed Millie's heart, where it struggled to beat against the pressure. "Are we still doing the party?"

"Yeah, sure," Travis said. "I just forgot my mother usually hosts it."

"Travis," she said, a bit exasperated. "I don't want to step on her toes."

"You're not," he said, glancing at her as they walked down a pair of dirt tire tracks. "I talked to her about it last night. She said she couldn't wait, though she did request we have steak of some kind."

They hadn't talked about the menu at all, but Millie knew Travis was teasing her when he shot her that devilish smile that made her whole being light up.

"Right," she said sarcastically. "I think you're the one requesting steak of some kind."

He chuckled, and she sure did like this more relaxed version of him. "I do love steak."

"That's something I already knew," she said. "Tell me something I don't."

"I built the bridges out here," he said, nodding toward the path ahead of them as they left the crude road they'd been walking on. The ranch behind them disappeared completely as they entered the trees.

The rushing of the river filled her ears, and Millie felt like she'd entered a whole new world. "Wow," she said, glancing up and wondering what these trees would look like in the full beauty of spring or summer.

Right now, they were kind of brown and a bit bare, but still beautiful.

"There she is," Travis said, nodding to the elegant walkway that went across the bridge. "That's the Wright's land over there," he added. "The river is the boundary between our properties."

"It's an arch," Millie said. "It's *so* beautiful." And so romantic. She wanted to kiss him on that bridge so badly, and she practically skipped onto it. "How do you build a bridge over water, anyway?"

"Carefully," Travis said with a grin. He joined her more slowly, his cowboy boots making a more clunky noise on the wood. "And scaffolding."

Millie leaned against the railing and watched the water flow beneath her and down the river. The air smelled clean and crisp, and she took a deep breath.

"You wanna tell me something I don't know?" Travis asked. "Like maybe why you're really here?"

Millie's heart skipped a beat, and she opened her mouth to ask him out.

In that moment, she gained new respect for all the men who'd asked her on a date in the past, because wow. It was not easy to find the right words and put them in the right order. She ended up just standing there, her mouth open with nothing coming out.

CHAPTER THIRTEEN

Travis sure did like Millie when she looked like she'd been smacked by a frying pan. He chuckled, and that seemed to break her out of the trance she'd fallen into. She turned away from him and tucked her hair behind her ear. "Do you want me to go?"

"Not at all." Travis rested his elbows against the railing and leaned over too. His back complained a little bit, but it was only one-thirty, and he wouldn't be dead on his feet for a few more hours.

Millie wore a cute pair of khaki shorts and a blue blouse that made her eyes seem more alive than ever. She fiddled with that hair again, and Travis really wanted to do it for her, cup her face in his hands, and kiss her.

Instead, he stood there and waited for her to say what she'd come to say—and it wasn't that she'd brought the tree skirt.

"It's Friday night," she said. "And I was wondering if you had any plans."

Thinking fast, Travis said, "It's fish fry night at The Ale House. Did you want to come with me?" He stepped over to her and put his arm around her waist, tucking her right against his side. Everything inside him aligned, and he took a deep breath of her hair. She smelled like pineapple and vanilla, and his eyes drifted closed in bliss.

"Yes, cowboy," she said. "I'd like to go out with you."

"Sorry," he murmured. "I probably should've realized I needed to ask you out for Friday night."

"I'm willing to overlook it this one time," Millie said. "I mean, you haven't been out with anyone in four years." She giggled and wrapped her arms around his waist too.

"Oh, wow," he said. "Throwing that in my face."

"We could go out to the bat cave after dinner," she said, still gazing at the water. "Lay on our backs and look up at the stars."

"Baby, if I lay down, I'm falling asleep," he said, thinking that lying beside Millie while he slept sounded like a version of heaven he really wanted to experience.

"Even to look at the stars?" Her voice had a bit of pleading in it, and Travis found himself wanting to do whatever she wanted him to.

"Maybe if I get a nap this afternoon," he said, knowing he wouldn't be getting any shut-eye before dinner. "And maybe if you pick up a hammer and help me and Russ build a wall."

"Let's go, cowboy," she said, stepping away and cracking her knuckles. "I'm going to show you what I can do."

"Oh-ho," Travis chortled. "And what's that?"

"Come find out, baby." She grinned at him and skipped down the bridge again. Travis shook his head as he laughed, because she was just...the exact breath of fresh air he needed in his life.

He hadn't even known he hadn't been breathing properly. They walked back to the build site, and he clicked on his tool belt and flipped his hammer around like a juggling pin before extending it toward her. "Here you go, sweetheart. Wow me."

Millie took the hammer with a glint in her eye he hadn't seen before. She marched over to Russ and said, "Can you show me what to do?"

Russ looked up, surprise on his face that made Travis laugh. "I'll help you," he said, joining them.

"I've built stuff before," she said, barely glancing at him. "With a glue gun," she added in a mock whisper, and that got Russ to smile.

"Glue doesn't hold buildings together," he said. "You take these smaller boards I've already cut, and you nail them in where I've marked them." He pointed to the blue chalk lines on the studs he'd already put in place. "Got it?"

"Nail them on the blue lines," she said, glancing around. "Nails?"

Russ pointed to the bucket of nails, looking at Travis next. He sucked back the laughter threatening to escape and glanced away to try to control himself. Russ chuckled and shook his head as he moved back to the power saw they'd set up that morning.

"When's the excavator coming?" he asked, grabbing a handful of nails and putting them in a pouch on his belt.

"Tomorrow morning," Russ said. "You promised I could do it."

"And you can." Travis started setting another stud into place and picking up the nail gun. *Pop, pop, pop,* and it was set.

"Hey," Millie said. "Why can't I use that?" She stood there with that huge hammer in her hand, staring at him with a look of disgust on his face.

"Baby, you can't just pick up a nail gun and use it." He grinned at her. "This thing has kick."

"I'll show you what has kick," she said, flirting right back with him.

Russ scoffed, and Travis cleared his throat. He wouldn't want Russ to have a flirt-fest with Janelle right in front of him either. Especially during working hours. So he got back to work, barely glancing at Millie as he set another stud twelve inches away from the first.

Straightening, he looked over, and she caught all of his attention as she hammered home a nail. She was so sexy in that moment, and Travis couldn't wait to be alone with her, the vast heavens spread overhead.

His heart kicked out an extra beat, popping like the nail gun did, and he was glad Millie was willing to drive to the ranch and insert herself into his life.

She's got to like you, he told himself, and that made his pulse skip around the way she had as she left the bridge. Millie ended up only doing one row of supports between the studs before she hung up her hammer and found a patch of shade to watch them work.

She didn't ask any questions, but she didn't sit and stare at her phone either. She just watched him and Russ as they interacted and worked. He was surprisingly comfortable with her eyes on him as he worked, and he finished putting up the last stud on the long wall and groaned as he stood.

"I'm done," he said.

"Yeah, I would be too if she was waitin' for me," Russ murmured. "Go on. I'll clean up out here." He grinned at Travis, who couldn't help grinning back. "And just be you, Trav. She obviously likes who you already are."

"Yeah," Travis said under his breath. "Thanks, Russ." He turned away, and reached for Millie though she was way too far away for him to actually touch.

She got up and dusted off her shorts. "Ready?"

"Yeah, we need a few minutes to put out the tree skirt, right?"

"Definitely," she said.

"I need to shower," he said. "But I'm starving, so I'll be fast."

"Take your time."

He opened the passenger door for her and guided her into the truck with his hand on the small of her back. He got behind the wheel and started back toward the homestead.

"Watching you work is amazing," she said. "You know exactly what you're doing."

"You know how to plan a party," he said. "I'm sure it's the same."

"Thanks for letting me hang out."

"Anytime, baby, though I'm not sure why you'd want to do that." He glanced at her and found her shrugging.

"I'm not exactly working right now."

"You want to work out here?" he asked. "We have plenty to do."

"Stuff I can do?"

"Sure," he said. "You can fill a trough with a hose, right? Toss out chicken feed?" He felt whiplashed between looking at her and making sure he didn't drive into the dog range.

"Yeah, I think I can do that."

"Great, you come out tomorrow morning, and I'll put you to work."

"Really?"

"Yeah, really," he said. "And I'll pay you too. We pay Brian and Tomas and Darren a bit more, because they're permanent ranch hands, but our seasonal workers get a hundred bucks a day. Eight hours. Hour for lunch—and I'll feed you."

"You will?"

"Well, I won't, personally," he said, pulling into the shed where they kept the ranch vehicles. "We have to walk a bit."

"What will you do for lunch tomorrow?" She unbuckled and slid out of the truck.

Travis met her at the tailgate and reached for her hand. "We usually make sandwiches or heat up leftovers."

"Will Russ cook tonight?"

"Doubt it," he said. "He's going out with Janelle."

"So sandwiches." Millie swung their hands like they were little children. "I like sandwiches."

"I sure do like you, Mills," he said, surprised the words were there and that he'd said them.

"I like you too, Travis. Oh." She spun back to the truck. "The tree skirt." She jogged back to retrieve it from the back seat, and they continued inside. "I'll get this in place while you shower."

"Deal." He dashed upstairs to get cleaned up, and while he wanted to hurry, he also wanted an extra moment to try to find his center. He felt better than he had in years, and he knew it was because of the last week with Millie.

After he'd scrubbed and dried and brushed and dressed, he hurried downstairs. Millie sat in the living room, the Christmas tree lit up and the skirt the perfect touch. "It's amazing," he said.

"We need to meet about the party," she said. "How about during dinner tomorrow? I'll bring it out here, or you can come to Momma's or we can go out."

"I've been craving the fried pickles at this place along the highway toward Boerne. Not that far, but yeah, south."

"Pickled Pig," she said. "They have the very best pickled onion slaw in the world."

"You like pickles?"

"Love them," she said, standing.

"I think that might be the first food thing we have in common," he said, grinning at her.

"Well, let's go see how we fare at The Ale House."

Travis reached for his nicer cowboy hat, set it on his head, and they went out. Dinner was an easy affair, with great conversation where Travis didn't have to come up with anything too hard to tell her.

She talked about her friend that she went hiking with every Friday morning, and Travis told her about how his dad had started giving him tools when he was eleven years old.

They drove out to Old Tunnel in the dark, but neither of them expected to see any bats. They didn't stay the winter in Texas, for the most part. A few did, he supposed, but the Mexican free-tail bats that came to Old Tunnel from spring to fall migrated back to Mexico in the winter.

He pulled into the dirt parking lot and got out of the truck. It really was dark out here, without headlights, porch lights, or street lamps. He managed to find Millie, and his eyes adjusted quickly to the darkness.

They only went out several yards, and Travis glanced around. "Wait, the blanket."

"I'll get it," Millie said, already walking away from him. He ran his hands down his thighs, because this was the moment he'd been waiting for.

There wasn't anyone else out here, and they had virtually no chance of getting interrupted. He could kiss her and kiss her—and he really wanted to.

She returned and spread the blanket on a bare patch of earth, sitting on it in the next moment. "You didn't get your nap," she said. "You gonna fall asleep?"

"Most likely," he said, joining her. "Do you think you can get us back to town?"

"In that behemoth of a truck?" She shook her head with a giggle. "No way."

"So you'll wake me up," he said, taking off his cowboy hat and laying down on his back. The universe opened up before him, and he took in a deep breath. "This is amazing."

"You live out in the country," she said. "Not a lot of light pollution out there."

"I don't slow down and experience the ranch that way very often," he admitted. "All I see is how much work there is to do."

"Mm." She nestled into his side, and Travis's heartbeat started booming through his body. "The stars are so beautiful. There's so many of them."

It looked like God had splashed white and gold across the navy-blackness of the heavens. "It's spectacular just before full dark, too," he whispered. "Sometimes you can still see orange and pink from the sun."

"Yes, I've seen that," she said.

Travis ran his fingers up and down her arm, her skin smooth. He had no idea how to make the next move, how to start this kiss he wanted so desperately. Not only that, he really hoped his last kiss wasn't a fluke.

"Oh, look," Millie said, lifting her arm straight up above them. "Mistletoe." She held a sprig of the holiday weed pinched in her fingers, and Travis could not believe it.

"Where did you get that?" he asked.

"I slipped it in your glove box while you were showering," she whispered.

He reached up and took it from her, turning onto his side so he was above her. He didn't know what to say, so he didn't say anything.

Leaning down, he cradled her face in his free hand and kissed her, his nerves settling the moment their lips touched.

He wasn't sure if this kiss was as good as the last, because for him, it was so much better. He and Millie breathed together, and he pulled away briefly before kissing her again. She moved with him, letting him control the pace, and he deepened the kiss, his emotions pouring out of him with every stroke.

Pulling back slightly, she whispered," Trav?"

"Yeah, baby?" He ran the tip of his nose down the side of her face, the scent and feel of her so amazing.

She didn't say anything either. She just guided his mouth back to hers and kissed him again.

CHAPTER FOURTEEN

Millie had never been kissed the way Travis was kissing her. He seemed to be in no hurry and yet urgent at the same time. She felt cherished, like he wanted to take his time and truly experience her.

She had time to run her fingers through his hair, along his neck, and across his shoulders. She couldn't get close enough to him, and by the time he pulled away, Millie wasn't even sure where she was.

She kept her eyes closed, the cool air flowing past her overheated skin. Travis's breath cascaded over her neck, making her shiver.

"Cold?" he asked.

"A little," she whispered.

Travis settled back down and pulled her against his side, bringing the edge of the blanket up over her arms. She opened her eyes and saw those glorious stars again.

"That was worth the wait," he whispered.

Millie smiled, because this man was darn near perfect in what he said and did, and Millie couldn't believe she'd caught his attention. She also couldn't believe she liked him as much as she did. Or that she trusted him.

But he was nothing like her father. She couldn't imagine Travis walking out on his wife and children, moving hundreds of miles away, and barely remembering to send cards for special occasions.

She swallowed back the bitter feelings and told herself again that Travis wasn't like her dad. He was here, and he wasn't going to abandon her.

"I don't want to leave," he said, his voice barely reaching her ears. "But I have to get up early and get some stuff ready for this beautiful woman who's coming out to the ranch in the morning."

She laughed quietly into his chest and then pulled away and looked up at him. He had a smile on his face and his eyes closed, and he was utter perfection in that moment. "Thank you," she said. "You're not bad yourself."

"Oh, not bad, huh?" He chuckled, opened his eyes, and started to get up. She went with him, letting him fold the blanket. The mistletoe she'd stowed in the truck got tossed somewhere, and she didn't try to find it. They didn't need it anymore.

Back at Chestnut Ranch, Travis walked with her over to her sedan, and said, "I hate that you have to drive home alone."

"I'm okay, Trav."

He gathered her into his arms again and bent down to kiss her. This kiss didn't last as long, but it still stole her breath and made her giddy. "'Night, Mills." He fell back a step and then two, tucking his hands in his front pockets. With that head ducked, and that cowboy hat back in place, she couldn't see his face, but she sure heard the smile in his voice.

"See you in the morning," she said, getting in her car. She drew in a deep breath and pushed it out, holding back the squeal until she reached the gate and there would be no way for Travis to hear her.

She made it home and practically bounced up the front steps. One step inside the house, and she realized she didn't live alone anymore.

"There you are," her mother said. "Where have you been? I was just about to send your brothers out to find you."

"Momma." Millie entered the house quickly and shut the door behind her. Guilt hit her hard. "I'm so sorry. I should've called. I went out with Travis."

"I know," she said. "I called out to Chestnut Ranch."

Horror replaced the guilt as quickly as it had filled her. "You did?"

"Russ and I had a very nice conversation."

"Momma, I'm not seventeen years old anymore."

"No, you're not." Her mom pierced her with a glare that said she was still Millie's mother. "Which is why I expected you to call me so I wouldn't be sitting here alone all night."

"I'm sorry, Momma," she said. "It was bingo night at the community center. Didn't you go?"

"Of course I went," she said, as if not going would've been a travesty. "I simply just expected to see you when the van dropped me off."

"Sorry." Millie couldn't believe she was apologizing. She was thirty-four-years-old. And she really needed her own place.

THE RANCH EMANATED BEAUTY IN THE MORNING LIGHT, AND Millie smiled though it wasn't terribly warm. She kept her hands in her pockets while Travis took her over to the chicken coops.

"Okay, so I have a confession," he said, turning toward her.

"Ooh, I can't wait to hear it." She grinned up at him. "Wait. Do I have to give a confession too?"

He shook his head and chuckled. "Nope." He lifted his cowboy hat and rubbed his hand through his hair. "So I have a special...fondness for chickens." He looked down at the birds, the clucking starting to fill the air.

"They seem to like you too." Millie reached over and took his hand in hers. His gaze moved from the chickens to where their hands were joined.

"Feeding them is pretty easy," he said, squeezing her hand but not like he had when he was frustrated. This was a loving grip, and he led her over to a small shed that looked barely big enough for one person to enter. "The feed is in here. You just scoop it into this bucket, and then each feeder has a line on it."

He scooped the feed into a bucket. "There are gloves right there, if you want them. Then you just go in and fill up the feeders. If anything looks moldy, you've got to clean it out."

"Do I have to go into the corral with them?"

"Corral?" He burst out laughing. "Corrals are for horses, baby. These are pens."

Millie rolled her eyes, but she only felt sparks inside her body. "Okay, fine. Do I have to go inside the *pen*, cowboy?"

"Yes, baby, you do." He indicated another container. "We add one scoop of grit. Mix, mix, mix." He did it without gloves, but Millie wouldn't. She hadn't spent fifty dollars on a manicure to mix chicken feed with grit with her bare hands.

"And there's two feeders inside the coop too. Those need to be checked too, because we have some alpha chickens, and we want everyone to eat."

"Alpha chickens?" For some reason, that tickled Millie's funny bone, and she giggled, pressing in closer to Travis.

He gazed down at her, that handsome smile on his face. He must've been practicing it for years, because he had the sexy grin down pat. He leaned down and kissed her, and Millie didn't mind one bit.

He backed up sooner than she would've liked. He repositioned his hat, that awesome flush staining his cheeks. "You'll have to make a few trips, probably," he said, his voice a bit husky. "And you can give them corn if you're feeling generous. They *love* corn."

"Does that go in the feeder too?"

"The corn you can scatter on the ground in the pen. I usually put it over on the grass, so they have to hunt for it more." He indicated the grassy area off to the left side of the pens. With all the directions, Millie was wondering if she was in over her head. Who knew feeding chickens was so complicated?

"Then you check their water," he said. "Again, anything that looks dirty or anything gets cleaned. Fresh water added. There's a pump in the middle of the pen, and it has a hose. The water bowls detach from the fences, and you can walk them over, rinse and clean them, fill them, and reattach them to the fence."

He made it sound like she could do this, so Millie just nodded. "All right." She took the bucket of feed and grit from him and set it on the ground. She gloved her hands as he took a few steps away. "I have to head over to the dog enclosure for a bit," he said. "I'll come check on you in an hour or so, okay?"

"Will it take me an hour to feed the chickens?"

"Maybe?" He shrugged. "If you finish early, you can go right next door to the goats. They need fresh water too, and it's the same process."

"What do the goats eat?"

"Grass, brush, weeds, whatever they can forage," he said. "And we give them half a bale of hay in the morning and a whole one in the afternoon, just to make sure they have enough to eat."

"Hay." She looked around like a big, strong cowboy would deposit the hay she needed right where she needed it. Having been raised in Texas, she knew enough to know hay bales came in a many sizes, and she wondered what a bale meant on Chestnut Ranch.

"And they like raisins as treats," he said. He pointed to a huge bag in the tiny shed. "One scoop for all of them. You can toss those in too."

"Do I have to go in with the goats?" She looked down the row of fencing to where the goat pasture was. "How many do you have?"

"Thirteen," he said. "They're for meat, and you can feed them without going inside. Their water is on the other side of that hay manger, and if the buckets look nasty, take them out and clean them. Then fill them up."

"Buckets," Millie said, wondering if the hundred bucks she'd get for this day was worth it. But she was spending time with Travis, and she knew that was. "Okay, chickens and goats. And you'll be back in an hour."

He smiled at her, leaned down and pressed a quick kiss to her lips again, and said, "Yep. Call me if you need me, and Griffin should be out here to help with the hay in about twenty minutes."

"Sounds good," Millie said in a falsely cheery voice, and she bent to pick up the bucket full of chicken feed. Mentally, she knew she could kick a chicken should one of the alpha birds come too close to her. But she still felt a bit trembly inside as Travis left her alone with all the birds.

She opened the gate and stepped inside, the warbling of the birds actually sending a pulse of joy through her. The chickens didn't lunge at her and try to peck out her eyes, and she walked among them easily. The fences that held their feeders sported bright blue, plastic containers, and she checked to make sure everything was clean and dry in the feeders before filling them to a hand-drawn line.

Travis was right; it did take a few trips back and forth to make sure all the feeders were filled, and then she faced the coop. She'd been inside a chicken coop exactly once before, and it had not been a pleasant experience for her nose. She did like seeing the birds roosting, but the smell...

After drawing in a deep breath, she steeled herself and went inside. The feeder here looked great too, and she poured in the pellets and grit. Only a few chickens were inside, and they were definitely not the alpha birds. She took the water bin out with her so she'd only have to go back in once, and moved over to the pump.

Intellectually, she knew how to pump water. Momma had a hand pump like this in her backyard, but she hadn't used it in years. Millie wasn't even sure it was still connected to a well. But this one was, and Millie cranked the handle a couple of times before water came out.

And then the water just kept coming and coming and coming. She yelped as it flowed over her shoes, groaning when she realized she'd have to work the rest of the day with wet feet. She jumped back and pushed the handle back down, bending over to rinse out the water container that went inside the coop. She filled it with water before the stream faded, and she turned to return to the coop.

"Everything okay?" a man called, and Millie slopped water over the edge of the container as she spun back to the fence.

Griffin Johnson stood there, leaning against the fence like he was on vacation. He grinned at her like he'd seen her take a bath in the cold well water.

"Fine," she called back. "Is that pump always so gushy?"

"Oh, yeah," he said. "One pump and fill all the buckets."

"Okay," she said, thinking that was vital information Travis should've given her. She returned to the coop, exploding back out so she could breathe properly.

The rest of the watering went fine, especially now that she knew the trick with the single pump. She had trouble with the reattachment of one water trough, but thankfully, no one was around to witness it.

She stepped outside of the gate and looked at all the chickens, happily eating and drinking, bobbing around and clucking. They seemed so happy, and Millie smiled at them too. "There you go, guys," she said.

Then she faced the goats and took a deep breath. "All right. Time for the goatherd." At least she didn't have to go inside the pen with them, but she also had no idea how she was supposed to lift a bale of hay.

CHAPTER FIFTEEN

Travis grinned at the little girl holding the nails for her mother. Russ had brought out Janelle and her two daughters for a day on the ranch, and the mood was completely different than anything Travis had experienced before.

There were high-pitched voices, and laughter, and hammering. Work was getting done, and his brother looked so happy. Travis had always known he wanted a family, and working with Janelle, Kelly, and Kadence soothed the ragged edges in his soul.

No wonder Russ wanted to get back together with Janelle, and it certainly seemed like that was happening, if the eyes Janelle kept making at Russ were any indication.

"Hey, stranger," Millie said, and Travis turned toward her.

Panic skipped through him. "How long—what time is it?"

She wore those farm gloves, she had dirt on her face, and wisps of hair had escaped from her ponytail. She was incredibly beautiful, and Travis's stomach swooped. He couldn't really believe she was here with him.

Him.

"I have no idea," she said, shading her eyes as she surveyed the build site. "I got the chickens and goats fed and watered. Where do you need me next?"

"Right here." He swept his arm around her and pulled her into his side. "Well, not really, but this is nice too."

"Janelle Stokes," she said, watching the activity in front of them. "And she brought her kids. She must really like Russ."

"I think it's the first time he's met them," Travis said. "We haven't talked about it much."

"Yeah, you Johnson boys are kind of private." Millie grinned up at him.

"Yeah, well, sometimes..." Travis wasn't sure how to say was what on his mind. "Sometimes there's not much to say."

"I know." She turned into him. "Should I try hammering again? I mean, these *kids* are showing me up." Her eyes glittered at him, and Travis started laughing.

"No, we've got a date with a well," he said. He stepped away from her and approached Russ. "I'm going to head out to the east-two well."

"Good luck," his brother said, his gaze sliding past Travis to Millie. "How'd she do with the chickens?"

"Griffin didn't say anything, so I'm assuming good." Travis shrugged and turned back to Millie. She'd moved over to talk to one of Janelle's girls, and he twisted back to Russ. "I think I'm going to tell her about Dani."

"Oh, boy," Russ said, looking away from his work. "You're really opening yourself up to this girl."

"She's...special," Travis said.

Russ looked at Janelle, whose dark hair fell over her shoulder as she bent to put something in place. "I know what you mean."

"We'll talk later," Travis said, hoping his heart was still intact when he met up with Russ again that night. He walked back over to Millie, ready for the next step in their relationship. At least he hoped he was.

"So we'll take an ATV out to the well," he said. "Have you ridden one before?"

"I'm from Texas," she said with plenty of flirt in her voice. "And I have three older brothers. I've been on four-wheelers."

"When was the last time?" he asked, flirting right back. "I'm guessing you used something more luxurious around the golf course for transportation."

When Millie didn't respond immediately, Travis knew he was right. He slipped his hand into hers and pressed a kiss to her forehead. "I wanted to talk to you about a couple of things today," he said.

"I know, I know," she said. "The party. I brought my intake forms, but they're in my car."

Travis cleared his throat and ignored the barking dogs in the range. "It's not about the party."

"Oh," she said. "What's it about then?"

Travis realized in that moment that Thunder, Winner, and Cloudy had come with him, and he paused. "Y'all aren't comin'," he said. "Go back to Russ."

Winner cocked her head at him, and Thunder actually sat down. Cloudy looked up at him, eagerness in her eyes. But they couldn't ride the ATV, and he wasn't taking the side-by-side.

"Russ," he called back the way he'd come. "Whistle for the dogs."

He did, and they immediately turned and trotted back to him. Travis smiled at Millie, and she wore interest on her face. "My ex-fiancée's name was Danielle Foster," he said. "She left me because, well, I'm not a hundred percent sure the exact reason. I couldn't really believe anything she said by the end of our relationship."

"Okay," Millie said.

"In the end, I think she wanted someone who spoke more than I did." He drew in a deep breath. "Which was why I was a bit sensitive when you said I don't talk much. And I'm pretty sure she thought I was just...simple."

"I like simple," Millie said, and Travis really wanted to believe her. "Life is complicated enough, you know?" She put her other hand on his arm, and Travis liked the way she clung to him like she needed him.

"It is," he said, the echo of Dani's voice telling him she liked simple haunting him. "Anyway." He cleared his throat. "I don't know why I wanted you to know."

"Because you just want to be who you are," she said. "I get that. It's too hard to live with ourselves if we're constantly trying to be someone we're not."

Travis nodded, thinking truer words had never been spoken. And he'd work on believing that Millie liked simple, because she did hold his hand and kiss him like she liked him. So maybe it was true.

They arrived at the shed where the ranch vehicles were kept, and he took the keys for the newest and nicest four-wheeler from the pegboard just inside the door. "Helmet?"

"Are you going to wear one?"

"No."

"Then I'm good." Millie followed him to the vehicle, and he checked to make sure the tools he'd put in the bag on the back were there. Satisfied they were, he climbed on the vehicle first. She straddled the seat behind him, snuggling in really close and wrapping her arms around his waist. "Ready. Don't try to throw me off to prove I haven't ridden one of these in fifteen years." She laughed, and Travis turned his head to look at her.

"Hold on, baby."

She already was, but her grip on his body tightened anyway. It was a quick ride out to the well, and he dismounted and turned back to help Millie get down. "Here we are," he said.

"It's so pretty out here," she said. "Your whole ranch is simply amazing. How long have you guys had it in the family?"

Travis knew this bit of family history. "My great-great grand-father came to Chestnut Springs only a few years after the town was founded," he said. "The Johnsons have been here ever since."

He collected the bag from the back of the ATV. "When did your family come here?"

"I'm not as old blood as you," she said. "But my great-grand-father relocated here and set up shop as a butcher."

"Where's your dad now?" he asked.

Millie pulled in a breath, and Travis knew instantly that he'd hit a nerve. "You don't have to say," he said. "Forget I asked."

"No," she drawled, really drawing out the word. "It's okay."

Travis glanced at her and started toward the well. He wasn't sure what was wrong with it, only that the water being delivered to the horse pasture was a trickle of what it had been before. Sometimes debris clogged up the well, and he had an extendable rake he hoped would clear anything in there so he wouldn't have to go down into the well.

"My dad left when I was fifteen," she said. "Well, fourteen, but it was the night before my fifteenth birthday, and I didn't find out until morning."

"He left on your birthday?" Travis stalled and looked at Millie, pure compassion moving through him. "Mills, I didn't know that."

She shrugged, but the pain was right there on her face. "He called from wherever he was, but I don't remember anything he said. He sent cards for a few years, I think, but after that..." She trailed off and shrugged again.

She sniffed, and Travis wanted to draw her right into his arms and hold her tight. He did, stroking his fingers through her ponytail. "I'm so sorry," he said once and then twice. "What a terrible thing to have to deal with as a kid."

"I honestly think he thought we'd all be fine without him," she said. "Once, he did tell me that I was old enough to under-stand what was happening, and he hoped I'd understand." She shook her head and stepped out of his arms. "I didn't under-stand. I *don't* understand." A fierceness entered her face. "I went to therapy for a while, and I learned a few things that have helped me deal with the anger and resentment."

She rubbed her hands up and down her arms as if cold. It was December, but it wasn't terribly cold. Probably sixty degrees by now. "I'm still pretty bitter about it, though." She met his eyes, worry in hers. "Does that make me weak?"

"Of course not," he said quickly. "It makes you human."

"Are you still bitter toward Danielle?"

Travis thought about it for a moment. "Honestly? I'm not sure. I don't think so?"

"She hurt you badly enough that you didn't date for four years," Millie said. "You aren't bitter or angry or anything?"

"I think I just felt so foolish," Travis said. "Like, I should've been able to see the signs that she wasn't happy, you know?"

"What kind of signs?"

Travis dropped the bag next to the well and looked down into it. Darkness didn't allow him to see much. "I don't know, Mills. Just that she said she was okay with me 'just' being a cabinetmaker. Or that she didn't mind 'carrying' the conversation when we went to dinner. That kind of stuff."

He unzipped the bag and pulled out a high-beam flashlight, clicking it on and peering back into the well. "I have a hard time believing women now, as a result."

Millie joined him at the well. "Do you believe me?"

The light glinted off the water in the well, so it was there. It just wasn't getting delivered where they needed it. He really hoped he didn't have to find a broken pipe somewhere between here and the stables.

"Trav?" Millie ran her hand down his arm.

"I'm trying," Travis said, refusing to look at her.

Millie sighed and turned around, leaning back into the well. "Every man who's ever come into my life has left."

"Have they, though?" Travis asked. "What about your brothers? You said the other night that you stay in touch with them, and they help with your momma as much as they can from where they are."

"You're right. My brothers have been constant."

"We don't all leave our families," Travis said. "In fact...I'm wondering how you feel about having a family."

"Oh." The surprise in her voice didn't comfort Travis, and he bent to get out the expandable rake. It was made specifically to comb through debris at the bottom of a well, where he could then scoop it out with the expandable rod with a scoop at the end of it.

"Haven't thought about it *oh*, or *oh*, I don't want to talk about it, or *oh*, I don't want kids."

"Oh, like I just wasn't expecting that question." She watched him pull out the rake, and Travis didn't dare look at her. He'd asked, and he couldn't take the words back.

"I'd like a family," he said. "In case you were wondering. I liked growing up with brothers, but sisters would've been awesome too." He finally glanced at her, only to find her smiling.

"I've always wanted a big family," she said. "Lots of kids and grandkids to keep me company when I'm old." She shook her head. "I don't want to end up like my momma."

Travis didn't know what to say to that, but he sure did like that she wanted a family. At least they were on the same page when it came to important things. "Understandable," he finally said, leaning out over the well and extending the rake down inside it. "Can you hold the flashlight for me?"

"Sure." She took it off the ledge and shone it down onto the water. He felt and saw when the rake entered the water, and he clicked the rod out one more time. Then again, feeling for the bottom. He finally hit it and began scraping.

"Oh, yeah," he said. "Lots of debris here." He pushed it to the side closest to him, always raking toward him. "Branches, leaves. There's been so much coming down the river this year. We've had to rebuild a couple of bridges already."

"The Hill Country has a reputation for flash floods," she said.

"Yeah, and undergrowth is a real problem—at least for us." He couldn't feel a lot of debris anymore, and he added, "Okay, now I need my scoop." He pulled the rake up one click at a time. "Leave the light there, sweetheart. I'm gonna need it."

He looked at her, and their eyes locked. Time slowed, and Travis's emotions softened for this woman. He knew what love felt like, having been that deep in a relationship before. So far that he'd bought a diamond ring and set a date.

And he was definitely falling in love with Millie.

CHAPTER SIXTEEN

Millie sure did like watching Travis work. He was efficient and strong, and while he didn't say a whole lot, what he did vocalize was important. She hadn't expected the conversation about her father or the question about having kids.

"Got it," he said. "Let me call Darren." He pulled out the long, extendable rake he'd been using to clear the well and balanced it against the stones. "You don't have to hold that right now." He gave her a quick smile before lifting his phone to his ear.

Millie set the flashlight on the well and took a few steps away. It wasn't even lunchtime yet, but she thought she should call Momma too. She did, a stitch of worry working its way into her lungs when her mom didn't answer.

She didn't leave a message, but instead hung up and immediately dialed her again. If she didn't answer this time, she might be asleep. *Or she could've fallen*, Millie thought. *Or left her phone at home and gone somewhere.*

But her mother wouldn't do that. She wasn't supposed to drive, and Millie's anxiety pinched through her as the call once again went to voicemail.

"Momma, it's me," she said. "Call me when you wake up, okay?" She hung up and turned back to Travis, who'd also finished his call. He was shrinking the rake, and he glanced at her.

"All fixed," he said. "Ready to head back in?"

"Sure." She approached him, putting a brave smile on her face. Or what she hoped was a brave smile. "Should we go over your party during lunch?"

"All right."

"You don't have to look so terrified." She giggled and wrapped her arms around him, glad she could do so without a bit of trepidation. "I'll do all the hard work, cowboy."

"Mm." He abandoned the rake and took her into his arms. "I just want something simple, Mills."

"Oh, Travis," she said, tipping up to kiss him. She stopped with her mouth a breath away from touching his. "Don't you know by now that I don't do simple?" She smiled as she kissed him, only realizing too late what she'd said.

Travis kissed her back though, and Millie relaxed in his arms. He pulled away when his phone rang, but he didn't answer it. "Mills," he whispered, keeping her close. She tucked herself right against his chest and swayed with him as if they were back on the dance floor at his brother's wedding. She couldn't believe that had only been eight days ago.

"I really am simple," he said.

"I know," she said. "But that doesn't mean the party will be." She stepped away from him, seeing the concern on his face before he could wipe it away. "I wasn't talking about everything in my life when I said that."

"Okay." He nodded and bent to pick up the bag of supplies he'd brought with him. His phone rang again, and he picked it up this time, saying, "What, Russ?" before walking away.

Millie hoped the annoyance she heard in his voice really was for his brother and not for her. He strapped the bag to the four-wheeler and climbed on, scooting forward and making room for her behind him.

She clung to him while he finished his conversation, and then he sighed, a lot of the tension releasing from his shoulders. "What's wrong?" she asked.

"Nothing," he said. "Russ was just calling about the well and to say lunch was ready. He doesn't like it when I don't answer the phone and I'm out on the ranch somewhere."

"You're not out here alone," she said.

"Tell me which direction to go to get back to the homestead," he said, and Millie looked around. Travis started laughing, and Millie sure liked the sound of that. She liked the way his body vibrated, and she liked that she was completely in his care.

"That's what I thought," he said. "And we have to go west, baby. Which way is that?"

"Uh." Millie looked around again, trying to use the sun as a compass. But it was very nearly overhead, and she wasn't sure. "That way." She pointed to her left, and Travis shook his head.

"Lucky guess, Mills."

"Hey, I'll take what I can get," she said. The ride back to the barn where they kept the vehicles happened quickly, and she and Travis walked over to the homestead hand-in-hand. "Let me go grab my folder." She hurried through the house and down the front steps to her car, her stomach growling at the scent of whatever Russ had heated up for lunch.

When she got back inside, everyone was there, not just Travis and Russ. Rex, Griffin, Darren, Tomas, and Brian all crowded into the kitchen, ladling something that smelled like tacos into bowls.

"Taco soup," Travis said, taking the folder from her and replacing it with a bowl of soup with corn, beans, and ground beef in it. "You can sit by Janelle, if you want." He leaned closer. "I think she'd like that."

Millie spied Janelle and her two girls sitting at the dining room table, bowls of soup already in front of them. She went over to them and found sour cream, corn chips, and cheese in the middle of the table too.

"Hey, y'all," she said. "Can I sit by you?"

All three of them looked up at her, and Millie smiled. "It's good to see you, Janelle."

"Millie Hepworth." The woman got up with a smile on her face and hugged Millie quickly. "I knew you were back in town, but I haven't seen you."

"You run the biggest law office in town." Millie waved her half-apology away. "You don't have time to worry about me. Though, if you're planning a party, I'm your gal." She laughed and looked at the girls.

"Girls, this is Millie. Millie, my daughters, Kelly and Kadence."

"Ma'am," the oldest one said, and Millie almost died.

"Am I really a ma'am?" She looked at Janelle, somewhat horrified.

Janelle's laughter pealed out, and she pulled out Millie's chair for her. "I've been teachin' 'em to be polite to anyone older than them."

"Look who's talkin' like a cowboy now," Russ said, suddenly appearing at the table. He flashed a brilliant smile at Janelle, who ducked her head and tucked her hair. As a female, Millie recognized the signs that Janelle sure did like Russ, and she wondered how long they'd been seeing each other.

She wasn't going to ask. Her momma had taught her some good ole Texas manners too. "How old are you girls?" she asked instead, and she got the girls talking about themselves, school, and what they wanted for Christmas. The men at the table didn't say a whole lot—well, besides Rex—and neither did Janelle.

"Let's talk about the party," Travis finally said, bringing out the folder he'd taken earlier.

"Yes, let's," Rex said, getting up and leaving the table.

"Does he not want to have the party here?" Millie whispered to the others at the table.

Travis rolled his eyes. "He just thinks he's funny." He flipped open the folder, and Millie's nerves bounced through her body. Her intake forms were really for her own eyes, and she didn't want him looking at them. "I have no idea how to read this." He gave her a sheepish grin and pushed the folder toward her.

Millie had already made some notes about color schemes and where food and drinks could go, based on her previous visits to the homestead. "It's not that hard," she said. "I just need to know what y'all are thinkin' about food." She glanced down the row of cowboy across from her as Rex retook his seat, more soup in his bowl now.

"Pizza," he said at the same time Russ said, "Anything but pizza."

Millie smothered a laugh and made a note. No pizza. "It's a Christmas party, boys. Think holiday. Upscale."

"Upscale?" Travis asked. "You think we're upscale?"

"Yes," Millie said simply. "Just because you guys run a ranch doesn't mean you have to eat trash at your family Christmas party."

"Steak," Travis said. "My mother likes steak."

"Yeah," Millie said dryly. "I'm sure she's the only one." She glanced down at her paper. "I already have steak on the menu, Trav. What else?"

"Cheese fries," Rex said, not smothering his laugh.

Millie glared at him, and to her surprise, he sobered. His face turned red, and he ducked his head. "Sorry, Millie."

Travis elbowed him, and Griffin watched them all like they were a great comedy act. Millie hadn't realized she'd be doing the party planning meeting with a whole crew. Dealing with multiple opinions was always hard, and she'd rather it just be her and Travis.

"Potato bites would be easy," she said. "Rustic, but still a little bit extra, you know?" It was clear from the expressions on all the men's faces that they did not know.

"My firm had a party once where we had apple fizzers,"

Janelle said. "It's just apple cider with some popping candy in it, but it was festive and fun. That extra you're looking for." She smiled at Millie, and appreciation moved through Millie.

"Yes," she said. "Like that." She looked at Travis and Russ, the two cowboys she thought she'd get the best ideas from.

"Mills," Travis said. "Just set the menu. You know what kind of food we like, so make it...extra, and it'll be fine." He got up and picked up a few bowls on his way into the kitchen.

"Back to work?" Russ asked, yawning.

"If you want," Travis said. "We've only been in for thirty minutes."

The ranch hands got up, thanked the brothers for lunch, and left through the back door. Rex and Griffin moved over to the couches in the family room and lay down, plunking their hats over their faces as if the bright sunshine would keep them awake inside the house.

Russ laced his fingers through Janelle's and leaned real close to her, saying something that made her light up from the inside out. Millie wondered if that was how she looked when Travis said something delightful to her.

Probably.

She pretended to be engrossed in making notes about the party, but she was really just waiting for everyone to leave and for Travis to finish putting away the leftover soup. The moment he closed the fridge, she shut her folder and got up.

Without speaking, they seemed to move toward the more formal living room through the doorway, and Millie followed him toward the front door. "You really don't care what you eat at your party?"

"No, Mills," he said with a sigh as he collapsed onto the couch. "Just feed us something awesome. The house will be decked out, and the tree is beautiful. We'll all bring one gift for the others, and we'll eat a simple dinner together."

"That's all?" she asked. "What else do you guys do at your parties?"

"My mom usually makes us go around and say something nice about each other." He patted the sofa next to him, and Millie joined him on the couch. "So we can do that."

"What do you want the tradition to be?" she asked. "That's what's important." She curled into his side, glad her clunky boots had been left by the back door.

"A nice meal." His fingers went up and down on her arm. "One gift per person. Giving compliments. What else?"

"Games?"

"We sometimes play games on Thursdays," he said. "And us brothers hang out on Sunday evenings."

"Right." Millie sat up. "About that...would you be able to sneak away tomorrow? There's the bell choir concert, and I've missed going for the past ten years."

"No bell choirs in San Antonio?" he whispered as he leaned closer and closer to her. Before she could answer, his lips touched hers, and heat exploded through Millie. Travis kissed her for a good long while, and she was pretty sure he only stopped when they heard an alarm go off in the other room so Rex and Griffin wouldn't catch them making out.

She felt like he'd dunked her in lava, and she tried to smooth her hair down from where his hands had mussed it up.

"Travis?" Griffin called, and he got to his feet.

"Yep," he said, extending his hand for Millie to take. "We're comin'."

Millie let him pull her to her feet, feeling like her bones had been replaced with gelatin. Wow, that cowboy could *kiss*.

"The bell choir sounds amazing," he said. "I'll pick you up at six?"

"Mm hm," Millie said, because she wasn't capable of anything more coherent than that.

CHAPTER SEVENTEEN

Travis changed his shirt and went downstairs so he wouldn't try on a different one. It was a blasted bell choir concert, not a Presidential dinner. Millie had seen him covered in dirt, wearing his regular old ranch clothes. The shirt didn't matter.

"You changed again?" Russ asked from his position at the bar.

"Look," Travis growled, because he was already late to pick up Millie. "I didn't press you even once about Janelle. Don't ask me about the shirt."

Russ held up his hands in surrender. "All right. Sorry. It's just that you've changed three times now, and you should just be glad Rex and Griffin didn't come out this afternoon. That's all."

"You should be too," he said. "Rex texted me for a solid forty-five minutes last night about walking in on you and Janelle."

"He's got to get himself a girlfriend," Russ said darkly. "Maybe then he'd leave the rest of us alone."

"Heaven help that woman," Travis said, and the two of them laughed. "Sorry to leave you here alone this afternoon." A slip of sadness did move through Travis that they weren't doing their weekly brother get-together.

"I'm not going to be here," Russ said. "Janelle's making peanut butter bars today."

"Oh, wow. See if you can bring some home."

"I'll be able to," he said. "Apparently, every December, she and her girls make a treat at least three times a week. They take them to neighbors, to the firm, and now, out here to us." He grinned like he'd just solved the world's problems. "So I'll bring you one."

"Nice." Travis swiped his keys from the pegboard by the door. "I'll see you later then."

"Yep, later."

Travis hurried out to his truck, and he may have driven ten over the speed limit to get to Millie's by six. The bell choir concert didn't start until seven, but he knew he'd have to go inside and make small talk with her Momma.

Millie had also texted him a lot last night, and Travis wished he'd asked her out instead of letting her go home after a full day's work on the ranch. He'd learned quickly that she didn't like spending weekend nights with her mom when she had a "hot cowboy boyfriend."

Travis didn't know what was so hot about him, but he knew he'd been exhausted last night. He hadn't even thought to ask Millie to dinner. He'd paid her, and she'd left. Of course, he'd only been able to take a shower and lay down for fifteen minutes before the texting started.

Rex had been highly amused by Russ's renewed relationship with Janelle, and he'd seen them kissing yesterday. Travis didn't care. If Russ wanted to be with Janelle, he could be—and should be. He was glad his brother had worked out whatever had gotten kinked in their relationship, because it was obvious that Russ liked Janelle.

He rang the doorbell at Millie's and heard the cat inside yowling. For some reason, that made him smile, and so it was that he grinned at her momma when she opened the door.

"Travis Johnson," she said, just like she had last time he'd seen her. This time, though, Millie was right behind her.

"Ma'am," he managed to say while Millie squeezed past her mom.

"Momma, we can't stay." She brushed a kiss against her cheek. "Betty will be over in ten minutes. I just got off the phone with her."

"Did you check the stew?" her mother asked.

"Yes," Millie said, stepping out onto the porch with Travis. It was obvious she was in a hurry to go—and obvious her mother was going to do everything she could to keep her there. "It's all ready, Momma. Rolls are cut. Your medicines are in the pill box. Do *not* forget to take them."

"I won't."

"I've told Betty to check."

Her mother's eyebrows drew down into a frown. "Did you—?"

"Momma, the movie is already in the blu-ray player." She linked her arm through Travis's and turned as if she'd walk away mid-sentence. "Let Puddles sit on the couch by you, and you'll have a great night."

"Millie—"

"Bye, Momma." Millie marched down the steps, and with the way she had Travis's arm laced in hers, he had to go with her or lose a limb. He helped her into the truck and leaned into the doorway, trying not to laugh.

"What was that about?"

"Oh, she's been on me all day." Millie patted her hair and finally looked at Travis. "I need to get my own place."

He nodded, closed the door, and walked around to the driver's side. "Why don't you?"

"I need a few more jobs before I can do that," she said. "Although, I got a call today from the pastor's wife. She wants to do a big Christmas shindig for everyone who doesn't have some-where to go for Christmas."

"Oh, that's great," Travis said, suddenly feeling bad for the amount of money he had in his bank account. Yes, he'd had times where he had to worry about things like paying the rent and putting gas in his truck, but admittedly, not for a while.

"Yeah." Millie exhaling heavily. "So I booked that. I'm still waiting to hear about the vow renewal up at Chestnut Springs. And I've got your party, a birthday party in March, and now the church thing."

To Travis, it didn't sound like a whole lot. With only a few things on the calendar, she didn't seem like she'd be moving out of her momma's house for a while.

Maybe she could move in with you, he thought, and he had no idea where that idea had come from. Number one, that wouldn't happen unless they were getting married. Number two, he'd only been dating Millie for nine days. Not even double digits yet.

He shifted in his seat, unsure of what to say. He probably didn't need to say anything. "Where is this concert?" he asked, only to give his mind something else to think about. Because while Travis had never taken long to know what he wanted, even he knew it was too soon to start tossing around words like *marriage*.

Way too soon.

"The community center," Millie said. "I think you just missed the turn." She swung around and looked behind her, and Travis's nerves went ballistic.

"Yeah, I did," he said, slowing as he moved over to the side of the road. He flipped around, his fingers tightening on the wheel. "I was just drivin'. Not paying attention." He got them going in the right direction, and made the right turn that would take them over to the community center, which sat right next to the fire station.

"Confession time," Millie said, and Travis nearly yelped.

"What?" he asked instead.

"When I was a little girl, I wanted to be in the bell choir so badly."

He managed to force a chuckle out of his mouth. "Is that so?"

"But you have to be fifteen," she said. "And by then, it wasn't nearly as cool." She shrugged. "Maybe I should do it now that I'm back." She turned toward the window and added in a much quieter voice, "I certainly have time."

Travis had no idea what to say. She certainly didn't seem happy, and a new kind of thought entered his mind. He mulled over it as he pulled into the parking lot, realizing they'd both gone quiet.

He parked and held her hand as they went inside. They definitely hadn't had to leave at six for a concert at seven when the venue was only ten minutes away. She tugged him toward a hallway on the right, but it was in the opposite direction of the theater where the bell choir would be performing.

"What's down here?" he asked, the scent of something sweet meeting his nose.

"Hot chocolate tasting," she said.

Travis chuckled low in his chest. "I see what's going on here. You don't care about the bell choir at all."

Millie gave him the pleasure of one of her giggles, her grip on his hand tightening. "Of course I do. But it just so happens that the one and only night of the hot chocolate tasting is right before the concert." She turned around and walked backward, and Travis thought that was quite the feat considering the shoes she wore.

With wedges that lifted her at least four inches closer to his height, she'd paired the sexy shoes with a pair of jeans and a red and white polka dot top. She looked like she could be one of Santa's helpers in the most wholesome of ways.

"You're not going to try any, are you?" she teased.

"Sure I will," he said. "Anything that doesn't mix chocolate and coffee. I know people love that, but I sure don't."

"What about chocolate and raspberry?"

"Yeah, that's fantastic," he said, his mouth already watering.

"Then there's another food item we have in common."

Travis beamed down at her, and she switched back to walking forward. The room where the hot chocolate tasting was happening wasn't hard to find. Laughter spilled from the room, as did chatter and the scent that could only belong to chocolate. Travis got overwhelmed the moment they stepped inside, and he wanted to walk right back out when he and Millie were separated.

"Vote for your favorite on every table," a perky woman chirped. "One per table. Meet back here with your absolute favorite, and you get a whole mug of that one!" She made it sound like he'd win the lottery if he did what she said.

He took the paper and nub of a pencil from her and tried to rejoin Millie, but the blonde put herself right in his path. "We have to keep the traffic flowing the right way, Mister Johnson." She singsonged his name, and he blinked at her. He should know who she was, and he knew her last name.

Robertson. But whether she was Phoebe or Bella, he wasn't as sure. He watched Millie giggle, take her pencil and paper, and turn her back to him. She stepped up to the first table and started sipping from the plastic cups volunteers behind the table were handing out.

Travis frowned, but he did the same, moving to table eight, which was on the left side of the entrance. A quick glance told him this table had five samples, and he might not be great at math, but eight tables meant he'd be sipping forty different kinds of hot chocolate.

He wasn't sure why, but he really didn't want to. Maybe if Millie were the one holding the small plastic cup to his lips. Maybe if he could kiss her after she tasted the one she liked best, and then he'd get to taste it off her lips.

He made it through the first five samples and wrote the number of the one he liked best on a slip of paper before drop- ping it into the box. He wasn't sure what the point was. Was there a contest? Who had come up with cranberry hot chocolate with almonds? Because that one was *disgusting*.

The line stalled a bit before he could get to table seven, and he looked over his shoulder to find Millie. He caught a flash of her hair before the crowd swallowed her again, and he ducked out the nearest door.

"Sir," someone said, clearly meaning to stop him. He didn't care; he went through anyway. The hallway was just down from where they'd entered, and he drew in a deep breath. A measure of embarrassment tread through him, but he didn't know what to do about it. He didn't want to be separated from Millie, he knew that much. And he had eaten a lot for dinner, so he didn't want to sip hot chocolate alone.

Maybe you don't want to do anything alone, he thought, and there was his blasted brain again, betraying him.

Music came from down the hall, and he wandered that way just to see what else was happening at the community center. He admittedly didn't get off the ranch very often, and certainly not for town activities as often as he should. That was more Rex's scene, and Griffin might go along with him instead staying in the house they lived in together alone.

Flashes of light spilled out of the room, and it was clear there was some sort of disco ball inside. He took a peek through the doorway, and it was clear this was a teen dance. Not for him. He'd have been mortified had his momma made him come to something like this, but the few kids he saw seemed to be having a good time.

He continued down the hall, ready for the bell choir concert to begin. Then he could get home and get to bed. Seth would only be gone for another week, and Travis wanted to get as much done on the new dog enclosure as possible. They needed the space, and he wanted his gift for his brother to be done before Christmas.

He'd also thought of the perfect thing to get for Millie, but he wasn't going to buy it. He was going to build it, and he needed an hour or two in the wood shop every day to make that happen in time as well.

He leaned against the wall down the hall from the hot chocolate tasting, in plain sight should anyone come out and look to their right. Millie would notice he wasn't there soon enough. Wouldn't she?

The minutes passed, and Travis began to wonder if he should go looking for her. Around the corner, a sudden whoosh of air caught his attention. As did the voice that said, "Caroline, you can't just go into the community center."

"Sure I can," a woman said, her footsteps coming toward him. "The door was open and everything. Let's just see—" She cut off as she rounded the corner. Her dark eyes glittered with mischief and the few women she was with caught up to her.

"He'll do," she said.

"Caroline," he said, because he knew this woman. The Landy's were old Chestnut Springs blood, and he knew them even if he didn't have any reason to deal with them. Especially Caroline, who was easily a decade younger than him. Maybe a bit more.

"Caroline," one of the other girls hissed, but Travis didn't know her.

"If we have to be in this awful town tonight," she said. "We have to have some fun." She looked back at Travis. "One of you get the camera ready." She batted her eyelashes at him. "Travis, I just need a quick favor. It's for a scavenger hunt."

He felt trapped by this woman, and he probably outweighed her by a hundred pounds. "Uh, I should probably—"

"Two seconds," she said sweetly, producing his worst nightmare—at least when this woman was holding it.

A sprig of mistletoe.

Before he even knew what was happening, her lips were on his and her gaggle of friends were giggling. Something flashed, and then Caroline released him.

"Thanks." She went back the way she came, and Travis leaned against the wall, his breath coming in huge waves. He gulped at the air, trying to get enough oxygen.

He'd just wiped his mouth when Millie said, "There you are. Who was that you were kissing?"

CHAPTER EIGHTEEN

Millie's heart thrashed around inside her chest. When she'd seen the dark-haired beauty kissing her boyfriend, her first instinct had been to run. Then she wanted to gouge out her eyes. Then the anger had taken over, and she'd watched Travis struggle to breathe as if he'd just experienced the best kiss of his life.

She knew; she'd seen him do that after kissing her.

And now he'd gone mute.

Millie's fury combined with frustration, and she just wanted to go home.

"No one," Travis finally said. "It wasn't a kiss, Mills."

"Don't," she said. "I *saw* you."

"No," he said quickly. "No, no. You didn't see me kiss her. She kissed me, and it happened really fast. She was just doing a scavenger hunt thing."

"A what?" Millie folded her arms and cocked one hip. If he knew how long it took her to pull these jeans on, he wouldn't be kissing other women.

An alarm inside her started to wail, and Millie breathed in deeply, trying to silence it. He'd already told her that not all men left their families. And the very next day, he was kissing someone else?

Nothing made sense, but Millie couldn't hear him if she let the panic inside her drown out her hearing.

"I don't know," Travis said. "That was Caroline Landy, and she's insane."

"Why'd you kiss her then?'

"*I* didn't," he said, clearly flustered. He glanced around the corner where the women had gone. "They took a picture. They're doing some scavenger hunt thing, and she held up the mistletoe and kissed me in like, two seconds. I couldn't even move."

"Uh huh, yeah," Millie said. "I saw that part." She turned away from him and started walking. She wanted to go to the bell choir concert, but not with him. Not right now.

"Millie," he said behind her, catching up to her in only a moment. "Wait." He touched her arm, but she yanked it away. Her chest felt like someone had poured in an entire hill of angry ants and then bound her with an unyielding rubber band.

"Hey," he said gently. "You believe me, right?"

"I'm trying real hard to," she said, the storm inside her raging now. "I just need a minute. Please." She walked away from him again, and he let her go this time. Millie wasn't sure she liked that, but she probably wouldn't like it if he wouldn't give her any space either.

He said something behind her, but she didn't hear the words as she'd let the fury and panic and irritation swell into something that was making all of her other senses go on hiatus.

She passed the teen dance and the hot chocolate tasting and went out the front doors. She gasped as she did, because it was cooler out here and she needed the air to think. Why was her brain misfiring now?

It felt like only a few seconds passed before Travis joined her. He didn't touch her, and Millie was secretly glad he hadn't just let her abandon him. He was there; he hadn't walked away.

"I gave you one minute," he said. "Do you need another?"

She turned toward him and searched his face, trying to find something, but she didn't know what. "You really didn't kiss her?"

"No," he said emphatically. "I wouldn't do that to you." He looked angry and sorrowful at the same time. "Millie, come on. This is *me*. I couldn't even talk to you at the speed dating thing. I'm pretty sure the only reason you gave me your number was because we went out ten years ago. And then…" He let his voice drift off as he shook his head. "You have to know I like you a whole lot. Why would I kiss someone else? It makes no sense."

"No, it sure doesn't," she said, her mind moving slowly through the things he'd said. He simply looked at her while she took the time she needed to understand. "Okay," she said. "I believe you."

"Thank you," he said simply. "Do you still want to go to the concert? I think I heard them warming up."

"Do you?"

"Kind of, yeah," he said, but he sounded a bit on the miserable side.

"Why'd you leave the hot chocolate tasting?" she asked.

"I didn't want to go around that room with that crowd by myself. I felt…claustrophobic."

"I'm sorry." Millie reached up and gently removed his cowboy hat.

"Mills," he said. "You don't need to be sorry. *I'm* the one who's sorry. I should've shoved Caroline away. She trapped me." He dropped his chin to his chest. "I'm sorry. I'm no good in situations like that."

Millie lifted his chin. "It's not your fault."

"You really believe me?"

"Travis, if we can't trust each other, you should take me home right now."

"I trust you," he said.

"Do you? Just yesterday, you said you were *trying* to believe what I'd said about being satisfied with you." She knew he had a past to work through. Heck, she did too. And not finding him in the tasting room and then seeing him kiss that other woman… every insecurity Millie had about all the men in her life abandoning her had roared through her head.

He didn't answer, and Millie handed him back his hat. "I'm trying to believe you," she said. "And I think right now, that's the best we can do for each other."

"I'm going to go find her," he said. "She'll tell you what I did."

"Trav, that's not necessary." Millie watched and waited as several people entered the community center. "Come on, let's go get a seat for the concert. It'll fill up."

"You sure?"

"Yes," she said, because she didn't want to talk this to death, and he still wore an agonized expression. She also didn't want him driving all over town to find Caroline Landy—someone Millie didn't even know. Sure, she recognized the Landy name, but all of their kids were much younger than her and Travis.

He's right, she told herself. He wouldn't be having a relationship with someone ten years younger than him. And he had been nervous during their two minutes of speed dating. And he kissed her like he was falling in love with her, and maybe she'd misinterpreted the kiss. Everything had happened fast, and there had been those flashes of light.

They found seats in the theater right in the middle section, and Millie reached over and took Travis's hand in hers. His eyes landed on hers, and he lifted their joined hands to his lips and kissed her wrist.

"I'm sorry," he murmured again.

Millie just shook her head. "You never gave me a confession."

"What?"

"Earlier, in the truck, I said it was confession time."

"I didn't know that was a two-way game." He cleared his throat. "I would've squashed that."

"Oh, come on," she said. "Anything. Something you wanted to do as a kid."

He seemed to think really hard about it for a moment. Around them, the theater started to fill up. Her phone buzzed, and Millie took it out of her purse to see Momma had texted. She didn't swipe on the device to read the full text. Instead, she shoved her phone back in her purse and looked at Travis again.

He was watching her. "You don't need to read that?"

"Nope."

He looked like he didn't believe her, but he said, "When I was a kid, I actually thought I could be a professional fisherman someday. That was what I wanted to do. Fish. All day long."

Millie smiled at him, some of the awkwardness between them finally evaporating. "Do you still like to fish?"

"If I had time, I'd probably like it," he said. "Haven't been fishing for a while, though."

Millie leaned closer to him and dropped her voice to a whisper. "You know you're a billionaire, right? If you don't want to work so much, don't. It's not like you need the money."

He stiffened beside her. "The work has to get done around the ranch."

"Then hire someone." Millie wasn't trying to be cruel. "Honestly, Trav, you don't seem that happy out at the ranch."

"I am," he said, but his voice was hollow and a bit high-pitched.

"All right," she said. "It's not my place to say." She squeezed his hand. "I just want you to be happy."

"And I want that for you too," he said.

"What does that mean?" Millie asked, but the lights dimmed, and the first clear, beautiful peal of a bell filled the air.

She'd ask him afterward, though her idea of a romantic Sunday evening with him had withered the moment she couldn't find him in the tasting room.

Only a few minutes later, her phone started ringing. Even the buzzing was loud, and Millie pulled her phone out to silence it completely. "Momma," she whispered, so exasperated with her mother. She'd done the same thing to Millie when she'd been dating Mitch. Suddenly, she needed Millie there at night to help her swallow pills, as if Millie could do that. She couldn't seem to find anything when Millie had a date. When she didn't, everything ran smoothly.

She swiped the call to voicemail and glanced at Travis. "Let's go," she whispered.

"Yeah? Everything's not okay?"

Millie shook her head and stood up. She needed to talk to him, and she needed to get home. She wanted to enjoy the bell choir, but she couldn't. "Sorry," she said to the people next to her, and she stumbled over feet in her haste to get out.

Travis followed her, but she waited until they were safely in the cab of his truck before speaking again. "What did you mean about you wanting me to be happy?" Her stupid phone lit up again, and Millie heaved a sigh. "It's my mom." She swiped on the call, and practically bit out the words, "Momma. What is it?"

"We can't find Puddles, dear. I know how much you love that cat."

Millie actually didn't care about her mother's mostly blind and deaf cat. "Momma, ask Betty to help you."

"She is."

"Fine," Millie said. "I'll look when I get home." The cat was probably curled up on her momma's pillow. Or in the backyard. She ended the call and looked at Travis. Something inside her told her to let this go, but she couldn't.

"I just feel like you're…" He cleared his throat. "Unhappy living with your mother."

"I am," she said. "But I can't afford my own place."

"I know," he said. "Maybe you could…I don't know. What are you going to do when she passes?"

"Excuse me?" Millie asked. "She's not going to die any time soon." The thought actually made Millie realize she could be trapped in her current situation for a very long time.

"Let's say she does," Travis said. "Are you planning on staying in Chestnut Springs?"

It was like God Himself had switched on a light inside Millie's brain. "You're worried about me leaving town."

Travis shrugged and said, "Not really."

"You're a bad liar," she said, the storm returning to her chest. Tears pricked her eyes and, she shook her head. How had this night gone so badly, so fast?

"I live here now," she said, though the memories of her life in San Antonio were so much better than the life she had now. "I'm not going to leave, even after Momma dies—which isn't going to be for a while, by the way."

"Okay," he said. A moment later, he pulled into her driveway. "Millie, I didn't mean to upset you."

"We're both working through some things," she said. "I get it."

"Would you—?" He clamped his mouth shut and shook his head. "Never mind."

"No," she said. "Just say it." Though if it was something else hard, Millie might just need to stay in bed all day tomorrow.

"Would you consider working for Chestnut Ranch full time? It comes with room and board."

Surprise filled her. "What?"

"We have cabins on the road before the homestead," he said. "Two of 'em are empty. You could live there. Work the ranch." He shrugged. "Do your party planning in the evenings and on weekends. Well, our ranch hands rotate weekends on, and they get other days off during the week."

"And you have the authority to offer me such a job?"

"Sure," he said. "We always need more help on the ranch."

Millie chuckled, but it wasn't an entirely happy sound. "You're really not a good liar, Travis." And she was glad of that. Then she'd know when he wasn't being truthful with her. In that moment, she knew he'd told her the absolute truth about the kiss with Caroline Landy. "But I'll actually think about it."

Her mother came out the front door, Puddles cradled in her arms, and Millie sighed.

"I'll call you later," he said, leaning over to kiss her quickly. Millie still felt a bit unsettled when it came to their relationship, but tonight wasn't the night to hash it all out. So much had been said already.

She got out of his truck and hurried toward her mother as she tried to come down the steps. "Mom," she said. "No. Go back inside. I'm coming."

CHAPTER NINETEEN

Travis didn't sleep well at all after dropping off Millie. He kept getting startled awake by the nightmare of Caroline's lips against his. That three seconds had taken something from him, and he got angrier and angrier every time he thought about it.

He finally got up before the sun, which honestly wasn't that hard now that Christmas was only a couple of weeks away. He needed to get started on Millie's gift so he had time to finish it before the Christmas party.

She liked organization, and she worked at a desk, so he'd been sketching out a custom desk that would hold her papers, her files, her little bobs and bits, like paperclips and labels and all the stationery that she'd told him about.

He'd just put the coffee to brew when Russ came thundering down the steps. "Trav?"

"Right here," he said, stepping around the corner. "What's wrong?"

His brother was tucking his shirt into his jeans, and he looked freaked out. "Momma called. She said the kitchen is flooded, and she can't get ahold of Rex or Griffin."

"They're probably still asleep."

"Yeah." Russ swiped his keys from the drawer. "Want me to go alone?"

"No," Travis said. "Give me two minutes. I'll meet you in the truck." He left the kitchen and took the steps two at a time to the second floor. He changed quickly and bolted back downstairs. He switched off the coffee maker and said, "Come on, guys," to the dogs. His father loved Winner, Thunder, and Cloudy, and that would get him out of the house.

Russ waited in the driveway, and Travis lifted Thunder into the back of the truck before climbing into the cab. "All right," he said. "Let's go."

After the quick drive to town, Travis unloaded the dogs while Russ went up the front steps. A startled cry filled the morning darkness, and Travis nearly dropped Thunder as the other dogs ran toward the front door.

"Stay back," Russ said, turning. "Trav, everything is wet. Dogs out back."

Travis whistled at the dogs, and they came back toward him. "Out back, guys." He led the canines through the gate and into the backyard. He went up the steps to the deck and opened the back door. At least an inch of water sat on the ground, and Travis didn't dare go in.

"Mom?" he called.

"I'm taking them back to the ranch," Russ said. "Mom's already out front. I'm getting Daddy now." He moved through sloppy, wet carpet and down the hall to their parents bedroom.

"What happened?" Travis called after him.

He kicked off his boots and took off his socks. He rolled up his jeans and stepped inside. This was going to be a nightmare to fix, and he was suddenly glad Seth no longer lived in the master suite on the main floor of the homestead. His parents would move back in there, obviously, and Travis and Russ would make sure their house was dry and mold-free before they came back.

"Dad," he said as his father shuffled through the water, leaning heavily on Russ. "What happened?"

"Near as we can figure, the pipe burst at some point," he said. "Momma started the dishwasher before bed, and it gushed all night."

"All night," Travis said, gazing at all the water. It felt like a job that was way too big for him, and he felt the same helplessness at cleaning it up as he did about getting Millie to believe him that he hadn't wanted nor invited Caroline Landy to kiss him.

"I'll be back in a bit," Russ said. "We'll call a restoration company."

"Right," Travis said. "I'll work on getting as much out of the house as I can." He picked up the nearest thing to him—a dining room chair—and took it out to the garage.

His parents still had a car, but they didn't drive it much. He'd need the space for everything that currently had water soaking into it, so he returned to the house and found the keys for the pickup his dad hadn't driven since his horseback riding accident.

He propped the door open with a can of paint, and he started moving everything out of the house and into the garage. The table and chairs were easy for him to wrangle alone. Barstools went next, and then the garbage can. He spied the wet-dry vac and grabbed that, putting the discharge hose out the back door as he started vacuuming up the standing water.

The restoration company would do that, but Travis didn't want to slop through any more water. Plus, he wondered if he needed to pull the stove out or not. In the end, he left it, because they could pay someone with more skills and knowledge than he had.

He moved into the living room and picked up his father's recliner. His back protested, and he groaned as he set it back down. "Ohh," he said as his back spasmed. So maybe he wouldn't be lifting the rest of the furniture out of the living room.

Picking up a lamp, he took that out. The lighter end tables went too, but Travis didn't even try to move the recliner or the couches again. Russ would be back soon enough, and he could help.

Russ did arrive several minutes later, and he found Travis in the backyard with the dogs. "Coffee," he said.

"Bless you," Travis said, taking the cup. "You know, we really don't have time for this."

"We'll just call someone," he said. "But it was a good idea to start loading everything into the garage."

"Yeah." Travis sipped his coffee, feeling the caffeine move through him with lightning speed. "My back freaked out when I tried to lift the recliner. I did everything else I could."

"Let's finish it up, then," Russ said. "I can stay and meet the restoration guys, and you could get back to the ranch to get started with the dogs."

"Sure," Travis said. "You know we're going to have to babysit Daddy, right? He's going to think he can come out onto the ranch and work."

"I know." Russ sighed. "I already gave him orders to stay in the homestead. Then I texted Griffin and Rex, so they'd know he was there."

"Did they answer?"

"Nope."

"Must be nice to sleep this late," Travis grumbled.

"Why were you up so early?" he asked.

"I don't want to talk about it." Travis turned back to the house. "Help me with the recliner."

"Something with Millie?"

"What part of I don't want to talk about it do you not understand?" Travis shot him a glare. "But yes, something with Millie." Maybe he should talk through things with Russ. So as they moved the furniture out of the living room and continued clearing things away from the wet hallway in the bedrooms, Travis told him about the hot chocolate tasting, the escape, the kiss with Caroline Landy.

"Holy stars above," Russ said. "What did Millie say?"

"She was angry," Travis said. "*I* didn't kiss Caroline. I told her everything. I tried to explain."

"Do you think she believes you?"

"I honestly don't know," Travis said. "We tried to stay for the concert, but her mom kept calling. I don't think she likes Millie being gone at night." He sighed and stretched his back. "I need some painkillers."

He found some in his mother's kitchen, and he turned back to Russ. "Can you go back to the farm? I just want to sit here for a while."

"Sure." Russ gave him a quick smile. "Sorry about your back."

"It's fine," Travis said. "I'll eat here, and the pills will kick in. I'll do all the evening chores."

Russ lifted his hand and waved, and Travis heard him calling the dogs to come get in the back of the truck. With everyone and everything gone, Travis didn't have a whole lot to do. He went into one of the spare bedrooms and lay down, falling asleep almost before he'd even taken off his cowboy hat.

He woke sometime later, his phone ringing. He wasn't sure where it was, and he missed the call from Rex. He didn't feel too bad, though, because maybe Rex now knew what it was like to have a call ignored.

He got up and yawned, looking at his phone. It was past nine, and surely the restoration company would be open by now. Instead of calling his brother back, he called over to Oakwood Restoration and got someone on their way.

While he waited for them to arrive, he did call Rex.

"Hey," his brother said. "Just wanted you to know that you have the whole day off."

"What?" Travis asked.

"Russ said you've been stressed, and your back hurts, and we all think you should stay at Momma's today and even tonight. Just...relax."

Travis wasn't even sure he knew how to do that. And laying around his mother's wet house wasn't his idea of a relaxing day.

No, a day like that would have fishing in it, and time in the wood shop, and pizza.

Travis's first instinct was to tell his brother he was fine. Instead, he heard himself say, "Okay. You sure you guys will be okay without me?"

"Oh, yeah," Rex said. "Everything will still be here tomorrow when you get back."

"Thanks," Travis said.

"Yeah, of course," Rex said. "Okay, so I just need to know where you hid the key to the four-wheeler..."

Travis chuckled. "I didn't hide it. It's hanging on the pegboard in the vehicle shed."

"Griffin said it wasn't there."

"Griffin can't find his own head sometimes," Travis said, laughing afterward. "It's definitely there."

"Okay, I'll look again."

"Rex," Travis said, sensing that his brother was about to hang up.

"Yeah?"

"Thank you." He meant it, and he hoped his brother could hear the sincerity in his voice.

"Sometimes we just need a day to take care of ourselves," Rex said. "See you tomorrow, bro."

Travis hung up, glad Rex had been able to be serious for even a moment. Then he used his phone to order that pizza he wanted. His dad would have a fishing pole, and he'd go back to the ranch and sneak into his wood shop without thinking about the dogs he should be building a home for, or the horses he hadn't fed, or the mowing that needed to be done.

HOURS LATER, TRAVIS RAN THE SANDING PAD ALONG THE wood, the gentle sound of it so soothing to him. Forward and back. Forward and back. With everything smooth and cut, he could start putting the desk together tomorrow.

His fingers ached, first from being curled around the fishing pole for a couple of hours that morning, and then from all the measuring, cutting, and sanding. But it had been a good day. A very good day, with all of the things he liked most.

Except Millie, he thought. He looked at the pile of precisely cut wood. He'd put it all together and then carve it into something feminine and beautiful. He'd stain it and put on custom knobs, and it would be a stunning piece of furniture.

He did like Millie a whole lot. He didn't want to lose her, especially not over something as stupid as a scavenger hunt kiss from a woman way too young for him. The very thought had his fingers curled into fists again, and that only hurt himself.

He really did wonder if she'd stay in town. Her mother couldn't have much money, as Travis couldn't remember the last time the woman had worked. And Millie barely had any income to speak of.

"Maybe she'll come out to the ranch," he said to himself in the peaceful serenity of his wood shop. He'd like it if he got to see her every day during lunchtime. He could sneak away from his chores to go find her, kiss her in secret, and then they'd go right back to their jobs.

He thought of her living in the homestead with him again, but there was something not quite right about that scenario. He'd always assumed Seth would live in the homestead, but he'd moved next-door to Jenna's place. Isaac Wright had bought another house in town, and he'd be moving before the New Year.

Now, it seemed like Russ would live in the homestead, especially if things got serious with Janelle. She had a family.

"And a house in town," Travis told himself.

Millie's words about him doing something besides ranching ran through his mind. He couldn't believe he was seriously considering it, but he was. He loved the ranch. He did. But he felt overwhelmed by it. Swallowed whole.

He could inherit his twenty percent and hire someone, like she'd suggested. He did have plenty of money, and he thought about his day fishing and building something he'd pulled from his imagination.

He liked woodwork. Loved it.

"That's what you should be doing," he whispered to himself. Seth and Jenna would be back on Sunday morning, and maybe Travis could talk to his brothers on Sunday evening. Find out how difficult it would be for him to pull back on all the ranch chores. He'd hire someone to take his place.

Because he really just wanted to build things again. He didn't even care if he sold them. He could just give them to the people who had inspired them.

With his mind still churning, he swept up the shop and went back to the homestead. Along the way, his phone buzzed several times, and he found half a dozen texts from Millie.

At least she hadn't cut him out of her life permanently. Guilt hit him, because while he'd thought about her a lot today, he hadn't texted or called her. And he had a phone that worked.

Hey, she'd said.

How was your day?

Momma is driving me nuts. I've started looking for another job. Want to talk me through it at dinner tonight?

He had no idea how much time had elapsed between each text, because the next one said, *Okay, so you must be out on the ranch somewhere without service.*

Call me when you come in for lunch.

Never mind. I can't do dinner tonight.

That was all, and Travis looked up into the darkening sky. He wanted to see Millie, and he didn't. Or maybe he did.

He wasn't sure, and he hated the confusion the most.

Sorry, he thumbed out quickly. *I was working in my wood shop. Too late for dinner?*

I'm in a meeting, her response read. *Call you later.*

Travis entered the homestead, glad it was just him and Russ, who had made omelets for dinner. He didn't ask him how his day was, or seek to know more about Millie. They just ate, and then Travis went upstairs to shower. He waited for Millie to call and tell him about the meeting she was having in the evening, but she never did.

CHAPTER TWENTY

Millie had just stepped out of the shower when her phone rang. She hurried across the slippery tiles to get the call before it went to voicemail. Yesterday had been an exercise in frustration, first from not being able to communicate with Travis to having a two-hour long meeting that didn't end with her getting a signed contract.

But maybe this call was Chris and Kayla, saying they'd love to hire her to be their wedding coordinator.

The screen said Ramon Pedraza on it though, and Millie swiped the call on. "Ramon," she said, a bit out of breath. She'd already taken Momma on their walk, and the next item on her agenda was to get out to Chestnut Ranch and ask Travis for that job he'd mentioned.

His question about her status in town had hurt, for a reason she couldn't name. But she also had to face facts, and the fact was, she had no way to support herself in Chestnut Springs. The wedding planners in the area worked all over the Hill Country, and she couldn't travel that much. At least not right now.

"Millie," Ramon said. "Our admin meeting was last night, and I'm sorry, but we can't close the entire trail to Chestnut Springs for a private event."

Millie wanted to argue, but she knew she wouldn't win. "All right," she said. "Thanks for bringing it up."

"Sorry," he said again. "I mentioned the pool, like you said, but the rest of the team didn't think we could close a mountain."

The trail to the springs was hardly a mountain, but Millie kept that biting remark under her tongue too. "It's okay," she said. "Thanks for letting me know." Sighing, she hung up. She didn't bother to get dressed before she called Diane Toolson and relayed the unfortunate news.

"Then I don't need a party planner," Diane said. "What do I owe you for checking on that for me?"

"Nothing," Millie said, though she could use twenty bucks just to get a coffee and put gas in her car.

"Thank you, dear." Diane hung up, and Millie hated that she'd lost a potential client. This one was completely out of her hands, but still.

She dressed, put on her makeup carefully, making sure each line of eyeliner was exactly right, and curled her hair.

"Where are you goin' all dolled up?" Momma asked from her near-constant perch at the kitchen table.

"I'm going to get a job, Momma," she said. She could help her mother around the demands of the ranch, she knew that. Her heart wailed at the idea of going to her boyfriend and groveling for a job, but she'd done worse.

"What about Serendipity?" Momma asked.

"It's not really a job," Millie said. "I can do almost all of it online, and it's mostly just a title I have to make sure the other independent contractors who want to use Serendipity's facilities are scheduled and have what they need. Mildred has a staff for that, so all I do is communicate with the contractors so Mildred doesn't have to."

"You get paid, though, right?"

"Not until January," Millie said. "Everything is taken care of until then." And she'd wanted the coordinator contract, so she could use the facilities without having to go through a middleman. But she hadn't been able to get anyone to hire her for a fancy party or wedding that required the beautiful wildflower farms at Serendipity.

She swept a kiss along her mother's hairline, though the woman could be absolutely maddening, grabbed her keys, and headed out. She sighed from the safety of her car. She couldn't stay home with her mother for another day. Yesterday had been horrible, with nothing to do and nowhere to go. Millie had been tempted to make something up just to get out of the house.

She loved her mother, but she wanted to talk about the same things over and over, and she watched game shows from decades past. Millie needed something to *do*, and while she thought the work around the ranch might kill her, she knew she'd get used to it.

Her boots pinched her toes as she drove out to the ranch. She parked in the driveway and gathered her courage as close as she could get it. She managed to walk to the front door and ring the doorbell, but no one came to answer it. She could just see the Christmas tree she and Travis had set up, and its presence made her smile.

She turned around and faced the ranch. "Maybe he's out working on the dog enclosure." She knew where that was. And the chicken coops, the goat pasture, and the vehicle sheds. If Travis wasn't in any of those places, Millie couldn't very well start tromping all over the ranch.

No one was working on the dog enclosure that day. In fact, the entire ranch seemed to be asleep, and Millie wondered where everyone was. Because it was almost lunchtime, she went back to the homestead and sat down on the front steps. Surely she'd know when someone showed up.

Sure enough, about fifteen minutes later, she heard someone laughing inside the house. It wasn't Travis, but it was male, and that was good enough for Millie. She rang the doorbell again, and this time Rex Johnson answered the door.

"Oh, hey, Millie," he said, leaning into the doorway like he owned the world. He was so arrogant, but he actually wore it well.

"Hey," she said. "Is Travis here?"

"Nope," he said, really popping the P.

"Do you know where he is?" Millie felt like this day was turning out to be worse than yesterday.

Rex looked over his shoulder, as if he needed someone to tell him where Travis was. "Yeah, he went to town," he said. "Something to do with Gabby or Greta or something."

Millie's mouth dropped open. "Gabby or Greta."

"Yeah, just a sec." He backed up and called into the house. "When is Trav gonna be back?"

"Any time now," Russ said. "I hope. He's got the drinks for lunch." He appeared in the doorway that led into the kitchen, and he stalled, clearly surprised to see Millie. "Oh, hey, Millie. You can come in and wait for him." He glared at Rex. "Why you makin' her stand on the front porch?"

"I dunno," Rex said, opening the door wider. "C'mon in, Millie."

Millie did, feeling a bit like she was entering the lion's den. "Thanks." She ran her hands up and down her arms.

"Are you hungry?" Russ asked. "We're just having lunch."

"I'm fine," she said. "I'll just wait here." She sat down on the couch where she and Travis had kissed last week, hoping the other Johnson brothers would just go away. Thankfully, they did, with Russ reprimanding Rex under his breath. An argument ensued, but they took it into the kitchen.

Gabby or Greta.

Millie couldn't help the jealousy running through her the way the Chestnut River ran and ran and ran. Travis didn't return "any time now," but at least twenty minutes passed before she heard him come in.

A moment later, he entered the living room. "Mills?"

She got to her feet, suddenly so nervous to face him. "Hey."

"What are you doin' here?" He started toward her, like he'd take her into his arms and kiss her. Only a couple of days ago, that was normal for them. Everything felt like it had changed now.

"Who's Gabby or Greta?" she asked, stalling his progress toward her.

"Who?"

"Rex said you were in town with a Gabby or a Greta."

Confusion ran across Travis's face, and Millie wasn't sure if she should be relieved he didn't know what she was talking about, or angry. Honestly, she was both.

"I was just in town to go over some stuff with the restoration company," he said. "My mom and dad's house flooded."

"Oh." Foolishness filled Millie. "Where are they staying?"

"Here," he said. "Right here."

She couldn't tell if he was happy about that or not. "I rang the doorbell earlier, and no one came."

"Okay," he said. "Maybe they were out back."

Millie wanted to say his dad never went very far, very fast, but she wasn't sure what she was accusing him of, exactly.

"You never called me last night," he said.

"I wasn't sure if you wanted me to," she said.

"Why wouldn't I want you to?"

She shrugged, though her insecurities from last night were as fresh now as they'd been then. "You never responded to my text."

"You said you'd call." He shook his head and held up one hand. "Okay, it doesn't matter. I feel like we're on two different pages here. Why don't you tell me why you're upset?"

"I'm not."

"Millie, I'm not blind, and I'm not the only bad liar in the room." He cocked one eyebrow at her, but his beautiful smile was nowhere in sight.

"Fine," she said, letting some of her anger rise to the surface. "I want to know who Gabby or Greta is."

He blinked at her, and Millie hated this weakness inside her. "I don't think you're cheating on me, but—"

"Yes, you do," he said. "That's exactly what you think."

"I don't know what to think," she shot back. "Because you never answer my texts."

"I was in the wood shop," he said. "It has bad reception."

Millie folded her arms and looked at him.

"I'm working with Oakwood Restoration," he said. "Maybe the woman's name is Gabby or Greta? I honestly don't know. She was just at the house this morning, and I had to be there to go over everything. That's all."

"Oakwood Restoration," Millie said. "Yeah, the Kline's own that, and they have a daughter named Gabby."

"There you go," Travis said, but he was clearly not happy. "Can I go eat now? Did you want to eat?" He hooked his thumb over his shoulder, but Millie felt rooted to the spot.

She shook her head, needing to ask him about the job here before she put anything in her mouth. Travis sighed and took a step toward her. "Okay, look, Millie. I really like you, but I think we need to take a step back."

"A step back?" Her eyebrows shot up. "Why?"

"Because you thought I was in town seeing another woman, for starters," he said. He spread his arms wide. "Millie, this is all there is. The ranch, and my family. If I'm not working on one of those problems, I'm asleep." He frowned at her. "I really don't like being judged for something I didn't do, and I don't need to answer to you for where I am or what I'm doing."

"I never said—"

"This is all my life is. It's boring, and it's mundane, and sometimes there's no service to get texts." He drew in a deep breath. "So you know what? I think *I* need to take a step back."

His words rang with awful finality in her ears. She didn't know what to say to get him to stop glowering, and she really missed the smile she knew could transform his face.

"Okay," she said, because what else was she supposed to say?

He watched her march over to the front door and open it, but he didn't follow her to close it. She stepped onto the porch, the wind nearly knocking her down.

She made it to her car and backed out of the driveway, beyond glad she hadn't asked him about the job. She couldn't even imagine working around the ranch if they weren't together. She slowed as she approached the cabins, and she felt like something she hadn't even known she wanted and needed had been ripped from her.

Because for Travis, a step back might as well be labeled a break-up, and Millie wondered how she'd gone from excited to see him and talk about a job at the ranch to leaving without a boyfriend and without that job.

WEDNESDAY AND THURSDAY WERE SPENT WALKING MOMMA, getting Puddles out of the tree in the backyard, and looking for a job.

Millie missed Travis keenly, because trying to find employment was one of the most soul-sucking experiences of her life. Momma didn't seem to understand that she couldn't just fish five-dollar bills out of the pond in the backyard, and Millie really needed a break from her mother. Part-time work would be enough, she reasoned, and she'd applied for at least a dozen jobs, from those in a more professional setting like a law clerk, to those that had her handing drinks and brown bags of fast food out a window.

When Friday morning dawned, she put on her short hiking shorts as normal, set the coffee to brew for her mother when she'd wake up, and ran out to her car. She and Angela were staying closer to home today, and she stopped by Ang's house to pick her up.

"Enchanted Rock?" Ang asked as she opened the back door and dropped her pack in the seat.

"Yep." Millie gripped the wheel, trying to keep her optimism and enthusiasm up. She hadn't told anyone she'd broken up with Travis Johnson, because she didn't have anyone to tell.

The hike to the top of the pink granite dome was pretty easy, and it would only take them an hour. The view of the Texas Hill Country was spectacular from the top, and Millie thought she'd be able to see Chestnut Ranch.

Her thoughts had been consumed by Travis and his ranch since he'd told her he needed to take a step back. She wasn't sure how he'd gotten so deep into her heart so fast, but the more she thought about him, the more she realized he'd had a piece of her most vital organ for over a decade.

Yes, she'd left Chestnut Springs to take the job in San Antonio, because her relationship with a younger Travis hadn't been that serious.

"How's the boyfriend?" Ang asked, going straight for Millie's weakest spot, and she didn't even know it.

"Uh, he took a step back."

"Millie, no." Ang actually sounded upset. "I'm so sorry."

"Yeah." Millie gripped the steering wheel. "There's a long story. I'll tell it when we get to the rock."

"I love a good hiking story," Ang said. "What else you got?"

"Well, I'm looking for a job," she said. "And that's not been going well. It's like, everyone will take your application, but no one calls you back. And stopping by or calling them feeling like you're trying to sell them a really bad car they don't want."

Ang laughed, and Millie chuckled too. Because she was right, and they both knew it. "So where have you been looking?"

"Everywhere," Millie said, glancing at her friend. "Do you need a personal assistant? Secretary? I can warm up the clients for you."

Ang gave her a sympathetic look. "Sorry, baby."

Millie gave her a warm smile. "I know. I was just teasing. I'm sure I'll find something soon." Though the holidays weren't the best time to find a job, Millie wasn't going to wait another day. She wouldn't ask for time off, and she wasn't going on vacation.

In fact, she'd invited all of her brothers and their families to Momma's, and everyone except David was coming. Her only single brother had himself a new, serious girlfriend, and he was going to Christmas dinner with her family closer to Austin.

She pulled into the parking lot at Enchanted Rock, glad they'd chosen this easy, well-kept trail for today. She sighed as she got out of the car and started stretching. "What a week."

"Yeah, start at the beginning," Ang said. "Don't leave anything out."

Millie wanted to leave a lot of things out, including the part where she'd seen Travis kiss Caroline—though she really needed to reverse those two names. Travis hadn't kissed Caroline. Caroline had kissed Travis.

"Okay, this isn't the beginning," she said. "But I need help with this the most."

"Oh, I am primed and ready," Ang said. "Go."

Millie swallowed, because what she had to say was going to be very hard for her. "I might have...I don't know. Accused Travis of cheating on me."

To Angela's great credit, she didn't reprimand or chastise Millie. She just looked at her, and asked, "Well, did he?"

"No," Millie said with great conviction. "No, he didn't cheat on me."

And for the first time in her relationships with men, she realized that she'd been the one to walk away. "I think I need to call my dad," she said.

"Oh, this is going to be a hard hike after all," Ang said, and she almost sounded happy about it.

CHAPTER TWENTY-ONE

Travis sat at the desk in his room, adding one more thing to his list of reasons why he wanted to pull back on his duties around the ranch and go back to doing what truly made him happy—carpentry.

Won't have to get up early.

Seth and Jenna would be home in the morning, and he'd already said he and Jenna wanted to host their Sunday evening dinner and game night at the Wright's house. Seth's house now.

Travis had responded to the group text and said he had something he wanted to discuss with everyone. Seth had acknowledged it on the text string, but Russ had cornered him in the kitchen. Travis wasn't keeping it a secret, and it had been Russ who'd suggested making the list.

The foundation on the dog enclosure had been poured and cured, and he and Russ were confident they could finish the whole building by the New Year. So not Christmas, but Seth would still be surprised and excited.

Travis had put the whole desk together this week as well, sacrificing his sleep to make sure he could have time in the shop, alone. He'd been keeping up with his ranch chores this week, but he really wanted to pull back on those.

"And maybe starting Monday, you can," he muttered to himself. His parents had gone back to their house yesterday, after everything had been deemed safe and sound. They'd gotten new carpet out of the deal, and now they were just waiting for the home owner's insurance check to come in.

Not that they needed the money.

Travis added that to his list. He didn't need the money from his fifth of the ranch, though he did want to keep it.

He got up and went downstairs, the sound of the washing machine making him happy for a reason he couldn't name. Maybe because he had very little to make him smile now that Millie was out of his life.

He hadn't meant to push her completely away. But he certainly couldn't defend himself every time he drove to town for coffee and didn't tell her. He shouldn't have to have a reason to be at his mother's with a woman. Nothing had happened, and Travis didn't like feeling like he had something to hide when he didn't.

And he didn't like that she didn't trust him. That was the big kicker, and even if Travis missed her, he didn't want to second-guess himself or her all the time.

The homestead was empty, as Russ had left to get to work already, and Travis needed to go help. He took care of the chickens, goats, and horses before heading over to the dog enclosure. Russ already had them outside, and Winner came galloping toward him, barking her head off.

"Okay, okay," he said, laughing as she rounded him like he needed to be herded toward the dog range. "Winny, I'm coming already."

Russ stepped outside and took his cowboy hat off to wipe his forehead. "Oh, hey," he said. "I'm finished here."

"I got the other animals fed and watered," he said.

"Great." Russ took off his gloves and tucked them in his back pocket. "Brian just called in to say he and Tomas and Darren are headed out to the fields for the last mow, and Rex and Griffin went out to the cattle with salt."

"Awesome," Travis said, thinking he should come out to the ranch later than he normally did. "We're working on the framing today, then?"

"Yep, let's get as much done as we can." Russ clapped Travis on the shoulder. "How are you holding up?"

"About how you were at Seth's wedding."

"So you're one breath away from a total breakdown. Got it." He grinned at Travis. "But maybe only I should work with the nail gun today."

"Ha ha," Travis said. "Very funny." He cut a look at his brother out of the corner of his eye. "How did you...I mean, were you just going to let Janelle walk out of your life?"

"I don't know," Russ said. "She freaked out because we'd been dating for a couple of months, and I wanted to meet her kids. So yeah, maybe I would've just let her go?"

Travis thought about what his brother had said. He and Russ were a lot alike, but also very different. Because Travis didn't want to let Millie go. Now that he'd taken a step back, he wanted to push forward too. She hadn't texted or called, and Travis didn't know how to break the silence between them either.

He'd been working on the desk, hoping an idea would come to him about how he could give it to her and get her back into his life. Nothing had come to him, and he hoped everything would become clearer once he could talk to Seth and everyone else about pulling away from the ranch.

"Hey." Russ stepped in front of him, and Travis stopped and looked up. "What are you going to do?"

"I dunno." He took off his cowboy hat and looked up into the tumultuous sky. "I built her a desk for Christmas. She's supposed to plan our family party."

"Maybe you should just call her," he said.

"Yeah, maybe," Travis said, but he wouldn't be doing that today. *Maybe tomorrow*, he told himself, and he definitely made sure he got access to the nail gun as he and Russ worked to put up the outer walls of the new enclosure.

"HEY, THERE HE IS," SETH SAID THE MOMENT TRAVIS CAME into the homestead from the ranch.

Relief rushed through Travis for some reason. "Seth." He grabbed his oldest brother in a tight hug and patted him on the back. Seth chuckled and did the same to Travis. "How was the honeymoon?"

"Great," Seth said.

"Don't let him lie to you," Jenna said, lacing her arm through her husband's. "He was bored out of his mind."

"I'm not much for sittin' on the beach," he said. "Doesn't mean I didn't have a good time." He grinned down at her and gave her a quick kiss. "Now." He faced Travis. "Russ wouldn't let me go out on the ranch, because you two have something to show me. Where is it?"

"Yeah, let's go," Travis said, excitement building inside him. "Where's Russ?"

"He ran upstairs for a sec," Jenna said. His boots sounded on the steps, and he appeared in the kitchen a moment later.

"Ready?" he asked.

"Yep." Seth adjusted his cowboy hat, and grinned at Travis and Russ. "It's so great to be back."

"Yeah, but you live next door now," Russ said. "Remember?"

"Of course I remember," Seth said. "But I can literally walk across a bridge, and I'm here. I'm not far, guys. We've talked about all of this."

"Let's go," Travis said, because he was anxious to show Seth what they'd been working on.

"Did Trav tell you about his new girlfriend?" Russ asked.

"Russ," Travis said. "Stop it."

"New girlfriend?" Seth asked.

"Millie Hepworth," Russ said, and Travis decided to just let his brother do all the talking. Russ would anyway. "They were *so* cute together, and then he kind of freaked out, and he hasn't talked to her all week."

"Wow," Seth said. "*So* cute together." He nudged Travis as they walked, but all he could think about was Millie.

"Whoa," Seth said. "What is going on here?"

"We're building you a new dog enclosure," Russ said.

"Merry Christmas," Travis added.

Seth stared at the building and then stepped in front of Russ and Travis. "Wow, you guys." He looked at Jenna, his smile widening. "Thank you so much." He grabbed both of them and hugged them, and Travis hugged his brother back.

"Take me through it," he said, and Travis started detailing how they'd designed it to be a double-long kennel, with gates in between if they didn't need the room for more dogs.

"But we do," Russ said. "Janelle has seven of them at her place right now, and I swear we have more all the time."

"I just need to get training again," Seth said. "And then we can start adopting them out, making room for the new ones we get."

They separated, and Seth looked at the skeleton of the building. "This is so great. I can't wait to see the dogs too." Seth had always been so cheerful, and his energy was infectious.

"Guys," Travis said. "I was going to wait to talk to everyone about this tonight, but I want you guys to know first." He thought about Millie, and the desk he'd built for her, and the life he wanted to have with her.

"I love the ranch," he said, stepping through his brothers and looking at the building he'd designed. "But I want to go back to carpentry." He turned away from the partially finished dog enclosure and looked at his brothers. "I want to keep my fifth of the ranch, and I'll hire people to do the work. But I want to spend my time fishing and in my wood shop."

"And with Millie," Russ said, grinning.

"Maybe," Travis said. "I have to figure out how to make things right between us. But yeah. Maybe."

Seth's eyes were wide as he stared at Travis. "Wow," he said. "I wasn't expecting that." He took off his cowboy hat and scrubbed his hand through his hair. "Wow. The ranch without Travis." He pushed out a big breath. "I don't know what that's like."

Travis knew what it was like to suddenly be missing a spirit on the ranch that he'd counted on for so long. And it wasn't pleasant.

"I'll still be here," he said. "And in fact, that's the other thing I wanted to talk to everyone about. But I'll save that for lunchtime."

"Whoa, whoa," Russ said. "There's more?" He exchanged a glance with Seth. "What is it? Even I don't know this one."

"Lunchtime," Travis said, and he just smiled at his brothers.

LATER, RUSS BARELY LET TRAVIS FINISH HIS LUNCH BEFORE HE said, "All right, Travis has news."

"News?" Rex practically yelled. "I heard we already missed out on the news."

"There's more?" Griffin asked.

"Give the man a moment to talk," Seth said. He nodded at Travis, who really didn't like the spotlight on him.

"I think you've all heard that I want to pull back from the ranch. I still want to do a few things, mostly the building repair and that kind of stuff. But the real change is going to be in the living arrangements." He didn't dare look at Russ, though his brother had been spilling all kinds of secrets since Seth returned from his honeymoon.

"Living arrangements?" Seth asked. "You're moving out?"

"Yes," Travis said simply. "Because Russ is the foreman here, and he wants to be buried out by his favorite horse, and I think he's going to propose to Janelle in the next couple of weeks."

"What?" Russ practically yelled the word. "I don't think so." He folded his arms and scoffed.

"Okay, whatever," Travis said. "But when you and Janelle do get married, you should have the homestead. Seth is next door. And I...want to build a house for myself just inside the gate. There's a great patch of land on the river, and it wouldn't take that much from the horse pasture."

The silence that followed made Travis uncomfortable, and he glanced around the table, not truly meeting anyone's eyes. "Say something," he finally said.

"For you and Millie?" Russ asked.

"No," Travis said quickly, though he was a bad liar and everyone heard it. "I mean, maybe. I just need to figure out how to talk to her."

"It's not that hard, bro," Rex said, and Travis rolled his eyes.

"Yeah, okay, *bro*," he said. "We're not all you, Rex."

"Yeah," Griffin said, and Travis wondered what that was about.

He wasn't the only one as Seth said, "What does that mean?"

"Nothing," Griffin said, lifting his chin. But it was something.

"I feel like I've missed so much," Seth said. "And I gotta say, it's not a good feeling."

"Yeah, missing a harvest and a flood and us taking on a dozen extra dogs must be really hard for you to deal with." Russ rolled his eyes and burst out laughing at the same time.

Travis liked the joviality at the table, the sense of brother-hood he felt. Yes, he'd been quietly sketching plans for the small farmhouse he wanted to build with his bare hands, and yes, he'd been thinking about asking Millie her opinion, with the hope that she'd be living there with him one day soon.

So he definitely needed to talk to her, and sooner rather than later would be best.

CHAPTER TWENTY-TWO

Millie drew in a deep breath and looked out the windshield. She'd told Momma she was going to grab some milk, just so she could be alone for this phone call.

She hadn't spoken to her father in a very long time, but the nagging thought hadn't left her for over forty-eight hours now. Millie had had promptings like this before, and the only way to get her pulse back to normal was to make the blasted phone call.

She tapped and pulled up her dad's number. At least she hoped it was still his phone number. He hadn't tried to contact her either, and the birthday cards had dried up long ago.

The line rang and rang, and Millie's heart pounded and pounded.

"Hello?" her father said, the voice as familiar to her as if she spoke with him every day. She wasn't sure if she liked that or not.

"Daddy?" she asked, wishing her voice wasn't quite so high.

"Millie?"

"Yes," she said, clearing her throat.

He chuckled and said, "Wow, that's what the screen said, but I wasn't sure."

Millie didn't know what to say. She wanted to tell him about

Momma and find out if maybe he could send some money. Something.

She wanted to clear the air between them so she could move forward. So she could get past all of these tangled feelings inside her.

"Where you at these days?" he asked, and Millie blinked her way out of her own mind.

"Back in Chestnut Springs," she said. "Did you know Momma's really sick?"

"Oh, your mother's always been sick." He spoke of her in an off-hand way, like he didn't believe her sickness was physical at all.

"Dad, she has ovarian cancer."

"She—wait. She has cancer?"

Millie sighed, her annoyance already at an all-time high. "How—yes," she said, deciding mid-sentence not to get into an argument with him. "I moved home to help her, because the treatments have been pretty hard on her."

"I had no idea." Something scratched on his end of the line, and Millie paused for a moment. She heard another voice, but she didn't recognize it.

"Anyway," Millie said when her father didn't say anything else. "I don't really know why I called. I just felt like I should." She didn't want to ask him anything. She didn't want to feel indebted to him.

"How are the boys?" he asked.

"Good," she said. "What are you up to?" Maybe she could just have a normal conversation with him, the way she did Angela.

"Oh, just life," her father said, and that person spoke again. "Can you hang on, Millie?"

"Sure." She actually pushed the volume button on the side of her phone so she could hear better what was happening on her father's end of the line.

"I don't know, sweetheart," he said in a soft voice. "You'll have to ask your mother."

Sweetheart?

Mother?

Where was her dad? Who was he talking to? Did he have a new girlfriend? And why would she have to ask her mother something?

The line scraped, almost like he'd put his hand over it. Millie could still hear him when he said, "I'm talking to my daughter... my other daughter."

Other daughter.

The words sent ice straight into her bloodstream, and she started to go numb.

"I'm back," her dad said, and Millie had no idea what to say. "Are you there?" he asked.

"Yes," she whispered. "Who were you talking to?"

"Oh, um..."

"Dad, are you seeing someone?" Maybe she'd been prompted to call so she could talk to her dad about Travis. She thought of him at the ranch that Sunday evening, eating and playing games with his brothers. She wanted to be there so badly, instead of stuck inside her car in the grocery store parking lot, dreading the moment she'd have to go back to Momma's.

"Not really," her father said, a big sigh following. "Okay, so I have to tell you something."

"Okay."

"I got married."

"What?" The word exploded out of Millie's mouth. The only way she'd been able to deal with her father's abandonment was to know that he was as miserable as her mother. Because he was alone too. Wandering, not sure what he wanted in life.

But if he was married, he could be happy.

He doesn't deserve to be happy, Millie thought, unsure of where the poisonous thought had come from. It was so unlike her, but the bitterness and anger were right there, as always, on the back of her tongue.

"I got married," her dad said again.

"When?"

"Last year."

Last year. Last. Year.

Millie could not believe it.

"I was talking to my step-daughter," he said. "Ohana. She has to be close to your age."

Millie bit back a horrible remark, the tears hot in her eyes. She couldn't speak, because then her dad would hear how his happy, new family affected her.

"How old are you now, Millie?"

"I have to go," she said in a rush and hung up. She flung the phone across the car and let her tears fall. They were partly because her father was not a nice human being. And partly because Millie wanted him to be. And mostly because she didn't want to be this upset about a man who'd left her twenty years ago.

"Time to move forward," she said as she wept. And she knew she needed to do exactly that. Delete the phone number from her phone. Find a job.

Get Travis back.

Her sobs increased when she thought of him. She wanted to go to him right now and tell him about her father's new family. He'd hold her close and stroke her hair and tell her he was sorry. He'd make her hot chocolate and bring out cookies, and they'd sit together on the couch until Millie had absorbed enough of his peace.

She'd called to get some closure with her father, but she felt like at least a dozen doors were still open between them. Her phone rang, but she didn't even try to retrieve it from the floor on the passenger side. At least it still worked.

Watching people move in and out of the store, Millie felt completely removed from the planet. She'd only felt this way one other time in her life, and that was when she'd moved to San Antonio by herself and found that the apartment she'd put a thousand dollars down on wasn't available.

Not only that, but the owner wasn't reachable.

She'd sat in her car then too, crying and wondering what she was going to do.

She'd survived.

She'd survive this too. She just needed to find an anchor to hold onto—and she knew who she wanted that to be.

Travis Johnson.

Her phone rang again, and Millie bent to pick it up. She couldn't quite reach it and ended up straining her back as she stretched too far. She finally got her fingers around it to find a number she didn't have saved in her phone.

"Hello?" she answered, probably just in the nick of time.

"Is this Millie Hepworth?" a woman asked.

"Yes, ma'am," Millie said, smoothing her hair for some unknown reason. The woman wasn't present.

"This is Chantelle Flood from Furniture Row. I'm hoping you're still available for our floor manager job."

"I am," Millie said, her heart beating erratically now for an entirely new reason.

"Would you like the position?"

"Yes, ma'am," Millie said. "I think I'd love the job."

Chantelle wore a smile in her voice when she said, "We loved you during the interview, and we think you'll do a great job. Can you come in tomorrow morning, say around nine?"

"Yes, ma'am," Millie said again.

"Perfect," Chantelle said. "And Millie, you don't have to call me ma'am." She trilled out a laugh, and Millie did too.

"All right," she said. "See you tomorrow." The call ended, and Millie gripped her phone tightly. She leaned her head back against the head rest. "I have a job. Thank you, Lord."

She wasn't overly religious, but she did believe in God.

Excitement built inside her, and she wanted to jump from the car and shout her happy news to the world.

In the end, she sent a text to Angela and got out of the car to go get the milk. As she walked toward the entrance of the grocery store, she copied the words she'd sent to Ang and put them in a text to Travis.

Could she send it? Would he respond? Would he be happy for her?

I got a job at Furniture Row! Floor manager. I start tomorrow.

The words were innocuous. Easy. Nothing about their relationship. Would she send them to someone who'd taken a step back from her? It wasn't like he'd said he wanted to step all the way out of her life.

"But he did," she whispered to her phone screen. "He *did* step all the way out of my life." He hadn't called or texted since they'd spoken last Tuesday. That was one giant step backward from where they'd been.

Part of that was her fault, Millie knew. So she sent the text and tucked her phone in her back pocket, though it had buzzed and chimed a couple of times while she'd stared at Travis's text.

She didn't allow herself to check her phone again until she'd bought the milk and returned to her car. When she looked, she had one message from Travis.

That's so great, baby. Congrats.

And four or five from Ang, with more exclamation points and more words of encouragement. Yet Travis's single text meant so much more than Angela's, and Millie knew then that she'd fallen in love with him.

We should talk about your family party, Millie tapped out to him. *When's a good time for you?*

She drove home, and he didn't answer. She poured milk into her mother's cereal-for-dinner, and he didn't answer. She told her mother about the new job, and he didn't answer. She showered and put her hair in curlers for her first day at her big, new job in the morning.

Travis simply didn't answer.

THE NEXT MORNING, MILLIE ARRIVED AT FURNITURE ROW curled and pressed and glossed. She walked up to the front door, but it was locked. Feeling stupid, she cupped her hands and looked through the glass.

There was no one inside. No other cars in the parking lot. Had she heard the time wrong? Unsure of what to do, she turned around and caught sight of another car just turning into the lot

Chantelle pulled right up to the curb. "Sorry, I'm a bit late, Millie. I'll go park around back, and you could follow me back there?"

"Sure," Millie said, digging her keys out of her purse again. She did follow Chantelle around to the back, where they both parked next to a door there. Chantelle unlocked it and held it open for Millie to enter first.

"It's good to see you," Chantelle said. "Let's go into my office." The room was a cluttered mess, but Chantelle hung her jacket and purse on a coat rack in the corner and sat in the chair behind the desk. "I have your forms here." She handed Millie a folder. "And today, we'll go through a few things this morning, and then you'll shadow me throughout the day. It's really not too hard of a job."

Millie flipped open the folder and found the usual forms for taxes and withholdings. "Okay," she said.

"The biggest question is what day of the week would you like off?"

"I'm sorry?" Millie peered at her.

"You work five days a week," Chantelle said. "It's a full-time position, with benefits. We need you here every Saturday, and we're closed Sundays. I'll work the other day of the week you have off. I just need to know which one."

"Oh." Millie blinked. "Is there one that's better than another for you?"

"No," Chantelle said. "We seem to be busiest the closer to the weekend it is."

"How about Wednesday?" Millie asked. That would give her a day off in the middle of the week, and that sounded good to her.

"Wednesday it is," she said. "You don't need to be here until nine-thirty. That's when our first salesman shows up, and the two of you usually get the floor ready for open at ten."

"Okay," Millie said, reaching for a pen. "Can I? Then I can take notes."

"Of course," Chantelle said. "But I have a paper here somewhere that outlines your duties too…" She started shuffling things on her desk, finally producing the paper she wanted. "Here it is."

Millie took it from her and saw the checklist, her heart warming. Prep floor sat right at the top. "What does prep floor mean?" she asked.

"Let's go do it," she said. "Then you'll be ready for—oh, wait. Never mind."

Millie looked at Chantelle, whose face colored. But she didn't know what the other woman was going to say she'd be ready for, and Chantelle ducked out of the office. Millie followed her, confused.

"Our finance secretary will get everything ready here," Chantelle said, having regained her composure. "But this is part of the floor, so you just check in with her. Her name is Andie Alonzo."

"Oh, I know Andie," Millie said.

Chantelle smiled. "Anything that's been moved, you put back. The night team isn't super great at keeping everything where it should be, and we sometimes have some teenagers who come in and like to make a mess of things. You know, a free activity on a Friday night." She rolled her eyes and picked up a pillow from off a credenza. "This goes on the chair here." She put the pillow in its proper place. "That's what checking the floor is. Usually you split the store with the salesman, and you'll rotate until you know how everything is supposed to look in every section."

"Okay." Millie looked at her paper, a bit overwhelmed already. How was she supposed to put things back where they belonged when she didn't know where that was in the first place?

You'll learn, she told herself. And it didn't all need to be memorized today.

"The next item says water cooler," she said.

"Yes," Chantelle said, moving toward a large desk in the middle of the store. "This is the customer service counter. We have a water cooler here, and one by the front door. It's the floor manager's job to make sure they're full and the cups are available for customers."

"Got it," Millie said. "Vacuum and dust the front displays."

"Those are the ones along the main walkway there," Chantelle said, pointing. "That's where we put our most expensive and newest items. They need to be clean for customers."

"Okay." Millie continued to move down the checklist, and when Colton Carlson came in, he and Chantelle started moving through the store, cleaning it up and setting things exactly where they went.

Millie checked the water coolers and cups, she ran a vacuum cleaner, and she checked in with Andie. She had a clipboard with the salesmen working that day, and which departments they were in. The customer service manager was also under her, and Teresa handed her a radio that Millie clipped to her waistband. She felt almost like the manager she was supposed to be, and she grinned around at the huge furniture store, feeling the rush of being in charge of all kinds of moving parts.

Colton unlocked the front door, which was also on her checklist, and Millie was surprised to see a couple enter almost immediately, almost like they'd been waiting for the store to open.

Her surprise morphed to disbelief when she recognized Seth and Jenna Johnson. "Seth?" she whispered to herself. He paused just inside the door, his new wife glued to his side.

Millie's pulse was back to that hard thumping, and she couldn't look away from Seth, even when Colton started talking to them. It wasn't her job to sell anything anyway. Match up the customer with the right salesmen. Make sure they were comfortable. Help with computers and delivery systems. Get them to the finance counter.

Seth and Jenna wouldn't move, and then they parted, and Millie knew why.

Travis stood there, searching the store for something.

His eyes met hers, and even from across the distance, Millie knew he hadn't been looking for something. But some*one*.

Her.

She could barely feel her feet as she started walking toward him, her heart positively leaping around her chest now.

CHAPTER TWENTY-THREE

"Is now a good time?" Travis asked, knowing from the shocked look on Millie's face that he'd surprised her. Good. He'd wanted to surprise her.

"I'm at work," she said.

"It's actually not ten yet," Colton said, and then he promptly disappeared.

"I'm going to go see if Chantelle has any doughnuts in her office," Jenna said. "Come on, Seth. She usually does."

"You had me at doughnut," Seth said, and he walked away with Jenna, leaving Travis alone with Millie.

Exactly where he'd planned to be. His pulse still ricocheted around his chest though, and Millie still looked like he'd hit her with a bolt of lightning.

"Hey, so I wanted to talk to you," he said. "And we only have a few minutes before you really will be at work."

"It's my first day, Travis," she said, and she didn't look happy to see him.

"I know," he said. "I called Chantelle last night." He took off his cowboy hat and ran his hand through his hair. He resettled his hat, reminding himself mentally about what he wanted.

"I made a mistake," he said. "Okay? I don't want to take a step back from you. At all."

"You don't?"

"No," he said. "You've always told me how great lists are, and I've been making one of the things I want."

Millie cocked one hip and folded her arms. "Is that so?"

Travis couldn't tell if she was flirting with him or not. "Yes," he said simply. "And I have one outside I'd like you to see."

She glanced around, but there wasn't another soul on the furniture floor at the moment. Chantelle had come through for him in a big way.

He half-twisted toward the door. "Will you come out?"

Millie looked like she'd rather go to Mars, then she nodded. Travis pushed open the door and held it for her, desperately wanting to take her hand in his. The desk he'd built for her stood down the sidewalk in the shade, and he went that way, Millie beside him.

She stalled after only a few steps though, and asked, "Travis, what is that?"

He continued toward the desk, where his list waited for him in the filing tray he'd built into the top of it. He stood next to it, admiring the craftsmanship. He'd stained the wood a nice, dark mahogany that made the wood grain stand out, and he thought the desk was beautiful.

Not as beautiful as Millie.

"This is your Christmas present, Millie," he said, putting his hand on the desk. He wondered if she'd accept the gift—all of the gift. Him included.

"You built me a desk?"

"It's not just a regular desk," he said, extending his hand toward her. "Come closer so you can see it."

She did, her steps slow and hesitant.

"It's a custom desk," he said. "With everything someone like you needs. Built-in filing tray." He indicated the sunken tray in the top corner of the desk. "A place for pens, paperclips, ribbons, folders, all of it."

He pulled open the top drawer. "The perfect depth for your lunch box. I was paying attention when you talked about your desk at your job at the golf course." He swallowed, because Millie was just standing there, and he couldn't tell how she was feeling from the blank expression on her face.

His nerves rioted, but he kept going. "This drawer is deep enough for files." The empty ones he'd put there swayed as he opened the drawer. "I didn't make it too big, because I know you don't like a big desk, and I called your momma, and she said it would fit in your room."

That was it. The whole speech had been delivered.

"Oh, wait," he said. "There's a paper here." He picked up his list from the sunken file tray, his fingers shaking slightly. "It's my wish list for Christmas. Do you have anything for me yet?"

Millie moved her eyes from the desk to him, and Travis could see something in her eyes now. Appreciation. Kindness. Love. Oh, how he wanted her to love him, the way he loved her.

"It's December sixteenth," she said. "I still have time to get you something."

He thrust the paper toward her. "This is all I want."

She took the paper and looked at it, bursting into laughter in the next moment. Relief rushed through Travis, because he'd take laughing over stunned staring.

"Did you decorate this?" She held up the paper. "It looks like my seven-year-old niece did it."

"As a matter of fact," he said, smiling at her. "A seven-year-old did make that. Janelle's daughter Kadence helped me. You should've seen my attempts. Russ said you couldn't even read the word."

"It's three letters," Millie said, looking down at the paper again.

"Yeah." Travis took a step toward her. "So, what do you think? Do you think I'll get what I want for Christmas?"

Millie wore that flirtatious look in her eye he'd seen plenty of times before as she looked at the paper and back to him. "Travis, I'm worried you think I'm something I'm not."

"I know who you are," he said. "I'm sorry I said I wanted to take a step back. I'm sorry you don't trust me yet. I'll do everything I can to fix that. I'm sorry I've been grouchy about working the ranch." He drew in a deep breath. "I've talked to my brothers, and I'm going to be hiring someone to take my jobs. I'm going back to my carpentry."

Millie looked up from the colorfully decorated paper that only had one word on it—*you*—and met his eyes. "Really, Trav?"

"Really," he said. "And you inspired that, Millie." He took another step toward her. She was so close now. So close. "I want to be better than I am, because of you. I want to build us a house in the corner of the ranch and live there with you, my wood shop out back and this desk in your office, that you use to plan parties or whatever. The only thing I want for the rest of my life, is you."

She ducked her head and shook it, her blonde curls bouncing. "Travis."

"I love you, Millie," he said, blurting the words out before she could tell him to stop talking. He couldn't see her face, and he didn't like that.

She sniffled, and Travis closed the distance between them, taking her into his arms and gently lifting her chin up so he could see her eyes. She was crying, and Travis found her absolutely beautiful.

"I'm not perfect," she said.

"You don't have to be perfect," he said. "Because you're perfect for me."

She looked at him openly now, and Travis felt the love moving through him before she said, "I love you, too, Travis. If you really want me, I'm yours."

"I really want you," he whispered, leaning his forehead against hers. "I'm sorry I—"

"Enough sorrys," she whispered, putting one finger against his lips and silencing him. "Kiss me, cowboy."

Travis chuckled, pure joy moving through him, and did what she said. Kissing Millie had always been a brilliant, powerful experience, but this kiss felt even more so than before. She loved him. He loved her. Whatever else they needed to work through, they could, because their love would lead them.

An alarm went off on Travis's phone, and he pulled away breathless.

"What's that?" Millie said, still tucked right against his body.

"It's ten o'clock," he said softly, breathing in the orange and vanilla scent of her hair. "Time for you to get to work."

Millie stepped out of his arms and looked at him. "You're somethin' else, you know that? Quitting on the ranch and getting seven-year-olds to help you with wish lists." She shook her head, that coy smile making Travis's stomach quake with desire.

"What time is your lunch?" he asked. "I'll bring you something, and we can talk about the Christmas party."

Panic crossed her face. "I have no idea."

Travis laughed, and Millie smiled at him. "Text me then, baby."

TRAVIS BENT AND COLLECTED ANOTHER WATER BOWL FROM A dog kennel. He smiled at Millie as he loaded it onto the cart she pushed. "You're not going to miss taking care of the dogs?" she asked.

"They're really Seth's babies," Travis said. "And I'm still going to be here. If I want to feed the dogs one day, I can."

"What about the chickens?"

"Funny you should ask about those," he said, moving down to the next kennel. The dogs were all still outside, so they had the building to themselves. He'd waited to do this chore until Millie had finished her first day at Furniture Row. She was radiant and absolutely perfect for him, and he'd spent the day on Cloud Nine, wondering how he'd managed to get her to look his way in the first place.

"But we'll be in charge of the chickens," he said. "I'm going to find someone to manage all the other stuff I do—the crops, the vehicular maintenance, the wells, the goats, and all of that. But I'm keeping the chickens."

Millie laughed and shook her head. "I knew you loved those birds."

"Yeah, well." Travis grinned and gave a half-shrug. "I'd like a dog of my own too. How do you feel about that?"

"I like dogs," Millie said, sobering. "So right before I texted you last night about the job, I called my dad."

Travis straightened completely, all thoughts about feeding and watering canines gone. "Really? Tell me about that."

She tried to shrug it off, but Travis could see how much the phone call had affected her, and it didn't seem like it was in a good way. "I don't know why I felt like I should call him, only that I felt like I should during our hike on Friday, and I couldn't shake the thought."

Travis didn't need to prompt her further. Millie would tell the story as they worked. So he picked up another bowl and waited for her to find the right words. He was actually glad she had to work to find them, as he often did as well.

"He got remarried last year," Millie said, her voice strangled. "And didn't tell any of us. He has a whole new family wherever he is."

Travis set down the bowls and stepped around the cart, taking her into his arms. "I'm so sorry, Mills."

She clung to him. "And I sat there in my car, and I cried, and all I wanted was you. I knew you'd do exactly this, and I needed it."

"Sorry I wasn't there," he murmured.

"Well, that blame is mine." She looked up at him. "You're not the only one who needs to apologize. I should've trusted you more. Of course I don't believe you kissed Caroline. I know you, and I *know* you wouldn't do that."

Love and acceptance filled Travis, and he nodded. "Thank you, Millie. And I'm not going to walk out on you or our family. Ever."

She nodded, her chin quivering again. "No steps back?"

"Only forward," he said.

She touched her lips to his, and Travis kept the kiss sweet and simple. Then he swayed with her right there in the dog enclosure as if they were back to dancing at his brother's wedding.

"Mills, will you plan our wedding?"

"Is that a proposal?"

He chuckled and swept another kiss along her forehead. "Heck, no. I'm not proposing in a dog enclosure."

She grinned as he released her, and they got back to work.

"But I would like to dance with you at our wedding," he said.

"I'll make a note of it," she said, something she'd said probably half a dozen times during her short thirty-minute lunch that day while they'd talked about the family party. "Okay, so tell me how you got all the way to quitting around here."

"Well, I'm keeping the chickens," he said. "And the building repair. So it's not really quitting."

"Your word," she said.

He gathered another couple of bowls and moved around to the next kennel. "Yeah, I know. I don't know. You said I was unhappy, and I don't think I'd ever thought about it before. I love being here, on the ranch. I love working with my brothers. I love horses, and dogs, and even the cattle. Sometimes." He flashed her a smile. "I don't want to leave this place or these people. I just don't like working as much as I do. And I got back in the shop to build your desk, and we started working on the new dog building, and I realized what I loved most."

"Carpentry," she said.

"Yeah," he said. "And my brothers have been awesome about it all, and yeah." He sighed. "It feels right."

"I'm happy for you," she said.

"Will you help me design the house?" he asked, feeling vulnerable and like she could reach right into his chest and scoop out his heart with her bare hands.

Emotion stormed across her face, and she nodded. "I'd love to."

Travis beamed at her. "Great. Now let's get these dogs fed so I can wash up and kiss you."

She giggled, but Travis was only sort of kidding. The dogs started coming back inside, which meant Russ was wrangling them up, and Travis did hurry to get them fed and watered then.

And then he got his kiss too.

CHAPTER TWENTY-FOUR

M illie bustled around the homestead, putting a silver candle on the center of the hearth, and then moving it to the end. A white candle took its place, and she lit them both, along with several smaller once nestled in the garland on the handcrafted wood. Travis had made the hearth, she'd learned—just as she'd learned dozens of other things about him in the past week.

What a great week it had been, filled with all kinds of things. Millie had been bored before, but now every minute of her life felt stuffed with activity, and she wasn't complaining. She took care of Momma in the morning and evening, and she worked all day at Furniture Row.

Chantelle seemed impressed that Millie had picked up the job so effortlessly, but Millie didn't think her duties were that hard. She had to make sure the store was welcoming and personable, that customers were happy, and that they had the people they needed to sell and finance furniture.

Chantelle had all of those people in place, and all Millie had to do was make them like her. She'd been doing that by taking a leaf from Janelle Stokes's book and making a new treat every day to take to work. The lemon bars had seemed like a real hit, and

Millie had made notes about who liked what so she could bring the right treats at the right times.

She plugged in a string of lights that lit the doorway into the kitchen, and she smiled at the huge bowl she'd put the punch in.

"After the fire," she muttered to herself, reaching for a box she then put in front of the gas fireplace. She flipped a switch, and those flames burst to life too. Candle after candle came out of the box, each of them a different size and shape. They were all scented like pine trees, and each had a wick that crackled like real fire.

With those lit, she stood back and admired her work. She'd brought in throw pillows, each one with a brand-new holiday cover on it. From Rudolph to Santa to poinsettias, the couches looked ready for a Christmas party.

She plugged in the tree in this room and hurried into the living room to do the same there. Russ had gone into town to pick up his parents, and Travis had gone for Momma, leaving Millie free rein to finish all the party prep.

"Dallas," she said, and the Bluetooth speaker she'd brought lit up with a blue light. "Play holiday favorites, volume three." Rex had a volume of three by himself, and Millie didn't want the music to be overwhelming.

With bells jingling, she laid out the silverware on the long table. Travis had helped her put in the leaf so it would hold the fifteen people coming for the party, and Millie had brought over the festive dishes. The plates were snowy white, not that it actually snowed that often in the Texas Hill Country. The bowls and cake plates had cute, bright bulbs on them, with a hint of a carrot nose every now and then.

Millie loved the dishes, and she smiled fondly at the tall glasses that brought a touch of elegance to the table as well. She couldn't help arranging the fresh flowers she'd picked up in town that afternoon, though a professional had already had her way with them. With all the candles on the table lit too, Millie turned her attention to the kitchen.

"Time for food," she said, opening the fridge and freezer. She scooped out all the lime and pineapple sherbet and poured the lemon-lime soda over it. With ice in the huge punch bowl, as well as a couple of drops of red food coloring, that was ready.

She'd ended up catering the food, something she'd put in place before her and Travis had taken their steps away from each other. They were back together now, closer than ever, and Millie's pulse fluttered with the mere thought of the cowboy she could call hers.

She checked the time, and said, "They should be here any minute," and she knew Preston Lewis was never late with his food delivery, even though she had ordered the food last-minute.

Sure enough, the doorbell rang in the next moment, and Millie half-jogged through the kitchen and into the living room to answer the door. Preston himself stood there, his hot-gloved hands holding a huge tray of something that smelled delicious.

"Millie," he said.

"Right through there," she said. "Thanks so much, Preston."

He went into the kitchen, and two more guys followed him, each of them laden with food. So maybe she'd ordered more than fifteen people could possibly eat, probably ever. Her philosophy was that it was always better to have more food than not enough, and she beamed at the long foil-wrapped trays now sitting on the bar in the kitchen.

"We've got the pies and cakes," Preston said. "And the rolls and salad, guys." His boys left to get more food, and he handed Millie a paper to sign. "How are you?"

"Good," she said as she signed. "You?"

Something flashed across his face, and Millie's compassion reared. "Holidays must be tough without Tammy," she said.

Preston nodded, his mouth set in a thin line.

"You and the boys run this yourself?" she asked.

"Yes," he said, looking relieved that she'd moved past his late wife so quickly.

"They seem like good boys," she said, handing back his pen.

The two teenagers entered the kitchen again, their hands full with more bags and trays. The scent of chocolate came with them, and Millie's stomach roared.

"They are," Preston said. "All right, guys. Let's hit the road." He tipped his cowboy hat at Millie, but she dashed over to her purse and pulled out some cash.

"Wait," she said, barely catching them at the front door. "Merry Christmas." She handed the teen closest to her the money, and he looked at it like she'd given him a winning lottery ticket.

"Wow, thanks, ma'am," he said.

"Merry Christmas, Millie," Preston said from the porch. She grinned as she closed the door behind them, hearing the garage door start to open.

Someone was back, and she hoped it was Travis with Momma. She knew Russ and the Johnson parents, of course. But she still liked having Travis as the buffer between them all. The glue that held her to this family that she was growing very fond of.

"Oh, my," Mrs. Johnson said, and Millie knew who'd arrived first. She hoped Momma wasn't being a pain, as her house was closer to the ranch than Travis's parents was, and he should've been back by now.

Millie stepped into the great room at the back of the homestead, where the party would take place. She loved the huge kitchen, the open dining room that bled into the large family room, and as soon as Travis showed her the blueprints for the house he wanted to build, she'd tell him she wanted a space just like this in their place.

Their place.

Emotion choked her, because she simply couldn't believe she might get her very own cowboy happily ever after at Chestnut Ranch.

"Millie, this place is magical," Mrs. Johnson said, stepping over to Millie and hugging her. "I do like this new tradition." She beamed at her and continued looking around while Russ helped his father over to the couch.

"We're here," Rex called as he and Griffin came in the back door too, and Seth and Jenna followed soon after, bringing the three dogs with them. Winner barked and barked, going up to every person as if to say hello personally.

Millie laughed as she scratched the dog behind the ears in greeting, still wondering where Travis was. Everyone kept telling her how great everything looked, and she caught Griffin trying to peek under the aluminum foil covering the trays.

The doorbell rang, and Jenna said, "That'll be Isaac and Luisa," and she went to get it. But she came back with more than Isaac Wright and his girlfriend, but Janelle and her two daughters as well.

"Hey, baby," Russ said, giving Janelle a quick kiss, and Millie thought they were so cute together. Utterly adorable. Probably perfect for each other, the way she and Travis were.

But still no Travis.

"Who are we missing?" Mrs. Johnson asked, her place in the kitchen cemented. Millie didn't mind. She'd got to plan the party, decorate the homestead, and prep everything. If Travis's momma wanted to run the show after that, Millie was fine with that.

And the brothers would clean up, so Millie couldn't imagine a better scenario than the one currently playing out in front of her.

If only her boyfriend were there.

"Travis," Seth said, finding Millie's eyes in the crowd. He'd already hugged her hello, as if she were a real part of the family now.

"I'll call him," she said. "He went to pick up my momma." She couldn't help the worry worming its way through her. She moved over to a quieter corner of the house and dialed. But Travis didn't pick up her call, which only made her feel like

Momma was having a meltdown somewhere, and Travis was trying to calm her down.

A moment later, she heard him say, "We're here."

Millie turned, relief filling her. She paused, watching Travis hug all of his brothers and hold onto his mother tight. She said something to him that made him laugh, and Millie fell a little deeper in love with him simply from watching him interact with his family.

He went over to his father, who had all three dogs trying to sit on his lap, and helped him to his feet. Then Travis looked at her, and whatever stress Millie had felt at making sure this family party went perfectly disappeared.

It didn't matter if the party went well or not. The food could be cold or disgusting. Rex could be too loud, or someone could give a terrible gift. None of it mattered, because they were there as a family, and Millie could feel the love radiating from every person in the house.

Travis came over to her and slipped one arm around her. "This is amazing, Millie," he said. "It looks and feels like a home now."

"Thank you," she murmured at the same time his mom said, "Okay, everyone. Let's do introductions, as there are some of us that might not know everyone." She smiled around at everyone, and Millie went with Travis to join the group gathered around the island in the kitchen.

Millie took her mom's hand in hers and squeezed. "Love you, Momma." She might have some ups and downs with her mother, but the truth was, her mother had stayed when things got hard. She'd stuck with the kids through everything. She'd taught Millie how to face hard things head-on and how to love fiercely.

"Love you too, baby," Momma said, and Millie wiped quickly at the tear that had escaped her eye.

"You okay?" Travis murmured, and Millie nodded.

"Yes," she said, smiling as Janelle introduced herself and her two daughters. Then it was Millie's turn, and she said, "I'm

Millie Hepworth, Travis's girlfriend. And this is my momma, Shirley."

Once the introductions were over, Travis's mom said, "Okay, time for compliments. Here's how it works…"

Millie listened, as she'd never done this before. It seemed complicated, but she soon got the hang of it. Travis's mom had started, and she'd given a compliment to her husband—and nothing "light," which meant she couldn't say she liked someone's hair or dress.

Then it had become her husband's turn, and he had to compliment someone else, and it had to be someone who hadn't gotten one yet.

He'd told Seth he sure did like how responsible his son was, and Seth now looked around the circle of people. His eyes landed on Millie, and she smiled at him.

"Millie, I sure do like how you've made this the most festive Christmas party we've ever had here."

"It's the *first* one we've had here," Rex said, rolling his eyes.

"Rex," Mrs. Johnson said, and he promptly shut up. So that was how that was done, and Millie almost started laughing. "Your turn, Millie."

Her natural instinct was to compliment Travis, but she said, "Kelly, I love how you've embraced the Christmas spirit with that dress."

Kelly beamed like she'd been told she was a beautiful angel, and she turned to her mom. "Momma, I think you're a really great baker, and I love that you've taught me how."

The game continued until everyone had a compliment, and then Mrs. Johnson said, "All right, Millie. Tell us about this food."

She did, and people moved to the table to find their place cards and pick up their plates. Travis kept his arms around Millie and said, "I think you're the most beautiful woman in the world."

Millie melted into his embrace and reached up and touched

his cowboy hat. "And you're the kindest, most dedicated, and handsomest cowboy I've ever met."

"Merry Christmas," he whispered before kissing her.

"Stop it," Griffin said. "Momma, they're kissing."

Millie pulled away from Travis, giggling as Travis told Griffin to grow up. It was simply the best Christmas she'd ever had, and she couldn't wait for many more with the Johnson family.

CHAPTER TWENTY-FIVE

A timid knock sounded on the door to Travis's wood shop, and he practically jumped out of his chair. No one ever came in here except him—and today, Millie.

"Hey," he said after opening the door.

"Hey, yourself, cowboy." She sauntered into the shop, which was lit up. Darkness had already fallen, and Millie had brought bags of burgers with her from town after her shift at the furniture store.

The family Christmas party had been a huge success, and Millie had hosted a second party at her mother's house on Christmas Eve, with two of her three brothers and their families there. Travis had met them both, and they were kind and accepting. Chris had even said, "Wow, Millie, how'd you get him to fall for you so fast?"

Millie had scoffed and swatted at her brother, and Travis had stayed silent. As usual. But really, he had fallen for Millie quite fast. He didn't care. He knew what he wanted, and that was that.

He thought about the diamond he'd bought that morning, during the jewelry store's after-Christmas blow-out sale. He wasn't sure when he'd use it, but he wanted to be prepared. Start making a plan. All of that.

They'd spent Christmas Day together too, first at her house with a fun brunch she'd made herself. Then they'd come out to the ranch and walked down the river and over the bridges while they talked about anything and everything.

And tonight, he'd invited her to his wood shop so they could look at the blueprints he'd started for the house.

"Did you build this desk too?" she asked, and Travis focused on the present moment. He had a tendency to get carried away with fantasies about the future, especially when Millie was with him.

"Yes," he said. "Everything in here. The shelves, all of it."

"And this is where you build everything too."

"Yep." He glanced around. "I thought I'd move this shop over behind the house, but Seth and I think it should probably stay here."

"How would you move a building this big?" she asked.

He loved her so much. "You don't," he said, grinning. "I'd have to build a new one and move the machinery and stuff."

"Okay," she said, swatting at his chest. "You don't have to laugh at me."

"I'm not," he said, though he did start laughing. "But it just means we won't have a wood shop in the backyard. You can still have an office in the house, though." He indicated the huge, square papers on his desk. "Let's look at the blueprints. I need your help, because I don't really know what a woman wants where." He pulled out the chair for her, and she sat. He stayed standing at her side, peering down at the plans.

"So the kitchen is here," he said. "Back of the house. I thought it would be good back there, because no one wants their front door to open to the kitchen."

"Smart," she said. "I love the open concept." She put one finger on the plans. "Kitchen table here, I like that. Big family room, I like that." She touched each spot on the paper. "Office up front. So I have to keep that clean."

She looked up at him, and Travis saw the glint of mischief in her eyes. "Please," he said. "You don't even know how to leave a desk messy."

"I can try," she said.

"Sure," he deadpanned. "Through that door is the master suite. Bedroom, sitting room, bathroom. Big closet—Jenna told me that."

"Jenna is the best," Millie said. "What's this?" She touched the bunk room, which was hard to depict on a flat drawing.

"Bunk room," he said. "For kids. Or a nursery, until we have more than one."

"With main-floor laundry too," she said. "Impressive. And this is not a small farmhouse, Trav."

"Sure it is," he said. "It's way smaller than this place."

"Is it?"

"You haven't been upstairs here," he said. "It legit has four wings and everything."

"So what's the second floor for this house?"

He pulled the paper out from under the one they'd been looking at. "It's much smaller. A small loft area, and then a bathroom with three bedrooms."

"That's still a ton of bedrooms," she said.

"You said you wanted a lot of kids," he said. "I didn't put anything over the garage though. Or the outdoor living space, which I'm still conceptualizing. Jenna has this great outdoor patio, and she said we could come look at it."

"Oh, wow."

"Yeah, and if you do that, then you can put rooms over the outdoor space, like a roof or whatever. I just didn't know how big of a family we were talking."

"This house has five bedrooms," she said. "That would fit eight kids, Trav." She looked at him, only seriousness in her face now. "Do you want eight children?"

"I don't want to say no if you do," he said.

Millie reached up and cradled his face, hers softening. "Travis, you get opinions about this. About everything."

Another dose of love moved through him. "Then, no, Mills. I don't want eight kids."

"How many?"

"I have no idea," he said. "But not eight."

"Four or five," Millie said. "That's what I want. And this house is plenty big for that."

"Okay," he said. "But you didn't say where you wanted things." He put the main floor back on top, because the second floor was just open rooms. "I'm talking kitchen island. Dishwasher. Stove. Fireplace. We can put it wherever makes the most sense to you."

The house was basically two halves, with the office controlling everything at the front. Behind that, the kitchen and family area spread out, and on the other side of the house, the master suite and bunk room took up the space. He knew they'd spend the most time in the family area, and he had the ability to make it exactly how Millie wanted it.

"So tell me," he said. "Not everyone gets to design their house exactly how they want it."

She took a deep breath. "Okay, I want a big porch on this thing."

"Okay." He picked up a pencil and made a note on a scrap of paper.

"And I think it makes the most sense to have the kitchen all along the back of the house here." She pointed to the back half of the house. "With doors to a patio here. We can eat out there."

"True." He sketched the doors right onto the blueprint and roughed out the patio. "So dining room here. I mean, it's not a room, but the table and chairs."

"Yes," she said. "And that flows into the living area. So the fireplace down at the end. We can put a TV above that. Couches facing that way. That would sort of separate the areas, though it's all one room."

"The patio could wrap around, and we could have doors up there too." He pointed where he currently had a window.

"Yeah, but then you can't put anything on that wall."

"Right." Travis left the window. "And I need help with the mother-in-law apartment."

"The what?"

Travis liked that she was surprised. He pulled out the bottom sheet. "It'll be an attached unit," he said. "This is what we're going to put in the backyard instead of the wood shop." He smoothed down the paper and looked at Millie. "I mean, if you want. I know you wanted a separate place from your momma, but I think she liked the ranch, and she does still need help." He shrugged, though he'd been thinking about her mother for several days now. "And out here, even when you're at work, there will always be someone to help."

Millie stood up and put both hands on his chest. "You're amazing. And I want her out here. But you know getting her to leave that house is going to take an act of God, right?"

Travis chuckled and rested his hands on Millie's waist, holding her close to him. "I know that. You know you don't have to work at the furniture store anymore, right?"

"I know that," she said.

Travis smiled at her.

"How long will it take you to build a house like this?" she asked.

"With the mother-in-law apartment?" He glanced down at the incomplete plans. "Three months."

"And are you planning on living there yourself?"

Travis's attention shot back to Millie, his heart throbbing in the back of his throat. "No. Wasn't that obvious?"

"So we'll get married in three months then."

"Is that a proposal? Because that is not how this works."

Millie's eyes gleamed at him, and he realized she was teasing him. "It's not?"

"No," he said. "No way. You can't ask me."

"Ouch," she said. "I've never been told no when I've proposed before." She tipped her head back and shook out her hair. When she leveled her gaze at him again, Travis's mouth went dry.

"How many men have you proposed to?" he asked.

"You'd be the first."

"No wonder it didn't go well," he said. "Because that was a really bad proposal." He kicked a grin at her and glanced toward his tool box, which had dozens of drawers holding the nails, screws, and other items he needed.

Including a diamond ring.

"I don't hear you proposing," she said.

"Maybe I have a plan for that," he said. "And you're ruining it."

Her eyebrows went up, and Travis remembered he had no plan. Nothing to ruin. He stepped back and released her, suddenly so nervous. He moved over to the toolbox and pulled open the top drawer.

The black box sat there, and he took a long, deep breath before turning to face her. "Okay, so there's no plan. But I happen to have this diamond I bought this morning, and I am in love with you, so..." He dropped to both knees and cracked open the lid on the box. "Millie, will you marry me?"

She sucked in a shaky breath and covered her mouth with both hands. Her gorgeous blue eyes watered, and she nodded. "This is what you do when there's no plan?" she asked, lowering her hands.

"Hey, you put me on the spot." Travis stood up, because the floor of his shop was cement and not comfortable.

Millie immediately cradled his face in her hands. "That was perfect. A surprise ring in the toolbox." She smiled, her eyes still watery. "I love you. Of course I want to marry you."

Travis grinned, ducked his head, and slid the ring on her finger. He kissed her, enjoying the way her fingernails scraped along the back of his neck and up into his hair. The kiss turned passionate quickly, and Travis didn't mind at all.

Millie pulled away soon after that though and sighed as she gazed down at her ring. "So, are you looking at a date in March?"

"You're a real slave-driver, aren't you?" he teased her. "But I suppose I can get the excavator rented to get the foundation dug. And yeah, with only chickens to feed, I can probably get this done by the end of March."

Millie looked down at the plans too. "Okay. Let's go over the mother-in-law apartment." In the next moment, she burst out laughing. "Who am I kidding? We're *engaged*! Let's go tell everyone we know."

CHAPTER TWENTY-SIX

Millie felt like frolicking through a meadow, bursting into a room where all of her friends were, and announcing, "I'm engaged to Travis Johnson!"

But as it was, her mother would probably barely smile, and the only other friend she really wanted to know was Ang. She texted her before she left the wood shop, and at the homestead, only Russ sat at the bar.

And he was not in a good way.

"Hey, Russ, we have—" Travis cut off as Millie practically squeezed his hand off. "What?"

Russ hadn't even looked up from his phone, and Millie nodded toward him, hoping she could say everything she needed to with her eyes.

"Russ?" Travis asked, and his brother finally looked up. If Millie thought cowboys could cry, Russ probably had been.

"Yeah?"

"Uh...what's goin' on?" Travis asked, gripping Millie's hand tightly too.

"Janelle—" He shook his head, anger firing from those dark eyes now.

Travis's feet shifted, and Millie hated the awkwardness in the room. She didn't know what to say though. She knew Russ, sure. But she wasn't going to give him advice, as she didn't know exactly what had happened. But something definitely had.

"Her ex came back into town," Russ finally said. "And she's unsure about us—again." He shook his head and looked down at his phone again. "I don't get it. I feel *so* sure about us."

"I'm sorry," Travis said. "What can we do?"

Millie marveled that he always seemed to know exactly what to say. She'd have said something like, *Maybe she just needs some time*, or *She has two girls to think about. Give her a few weeks.*

"Nothing." Russ got up from the barstool. "At least she waited until after Christmas, but now I feel like a royal idiot for all the gifts I got her and the girls." He shook his head, pure agony rolling off of him. "I'm going to go to bed. Wait. Do we have any of those steak bites left?"

He detoured over to the fridge and pulled out the container Millie had put the steak bites in. "Still a few," he said. "I'm taking these with me." He didn't bother to heat them up, and Travis didn't say anything as his miserable brother left.

He sighed as Russ's footsteps went up the steps. "I know he likes her, but Janelle has really jerked him around."

"He doesn't just like her," Millie said. "He's in love with her." She actually thought it was kind of sweet, the loyalty of his brother, and she sent up a quick prayer that Janelle could figure things out at home so she could be with Russ.

"Okay, so that was anti-climactic," Travis said. "I could call my mom?"

Millie grinned up at him. "Why was that a question?"

He shook his head and started laughing. "I don't know." He gathered her close and whispered, "Maybe this is just a secret for another night."

"Ooh, a secret engagement." Millie kissed him, and keeping their engagement a secret was almost as much fun as broadcasting it from the mountaintops.

❄

"Travis," Millie said as she entered the farmhouse he'd been working on non-stop for the last ninety-two days. "This is stunning."

"There are a few things that aren't done yet," he said, looking around at the space in front of them. Millie had watched the house go from a hole in the ground, to a two-story structure, to a building with walls and a roof.

She'd come out to the ranch nearly every day over the past three months, and she loved the house more and more with every visit. "I can't believe this is ours," she said.

"Office here," he said, leading her into the office. Her custom-made desk was already there, and Travis added, "You can pick out curtains and anything else you want."

"We have some great curtains at Furniture Row." She smiled at him. "I want to see the kitchen. I haven't seen the counter-tops yet." The custom cabinetry had been beautiful, and he'd ordered granite for the whole house. He'd made a custom butcher's block for the island, and Millie hadn't seen any of it yet.

She'd been busy planning the wedding, and then their honeymoon. Travis had never been out of the state of Texas, and Millie hadn't either. When she'd asked him where he wanted to go, he'd said, "How about the beach?"

And the warmest beach she could find in March was in Hawaii, so he'd funded their honeymoon to the islands. Travis had been funding almost everything to do with the wedding, and Millie sometimes felt bad about it.

But he didn't, and Millie didn't doubt his love for her. He said to do whatever she wanted for the wedding, and Millie had decided to take the cowboy billionaire at his word. She'd booked the flower gardens at Serendipity, and with any luck, there would be some early bluebonnets blooming, as well as some red poppies, or paintbrush, or something. If not, it didn't matter.

She'd ordered almost a truckload of flowers for the nuptials. So many, because she was going to wear them in her hair too.

Her dress had been tailored, she had the perfect shoes, and everything was set for their wedding in only three days.

"The kitchen," Travis said when they reached the end of the hall. A built-in desk could be seen from the front door, and Millie was glad she only had to keep that small area clean. Not that she was expecting many visitors. Just the Johnsons, and maybe Jenna—who was a Johnson now—and Ang.

"Oh, wow." Millie's breath caught in the back of her throat. The wall in front of her was loaded with windows, and the morning light coming through was simply spectacular. She couldn't imagine eating breakfast there with her husband, and her emotions overcame her.

"Everything is so beautiful," she said. She let go of his hand and ran her fingers along the countertop. It was a nice, gray granite that looked high-end. The butcher block was stunning, and Travis pointed to something in the corner.

"I sealed that," he said. "So you can still cook on it."

Millie moved over to the corner to inspect the carving there. It was professionally done, and it said JOHNSON in all capital letters. A T and an M sat above it, and tears came to her eyes.

"We can add initials for our kids," he said.

Millie sucked in a breath and faced him. "I love you so much."

"I can't wait until we're married and living here," he said.

She couldn't either, but there was still so much to do. "The furniture is going to be delivered tomorrow," she said. "So we'll have somewhere to sit and eat and sleep."

"Right," he said. "I'm picking up my tuxedo tomorrow too."

"Exciting," Millie said, smiling at him. "All of my brothers are coming the next day, and then it's wedding day."

"Three more nights," he said, leaning down to kiss her. "The house is ready, baby. I'm ready."

"Me too," Millie said. "I'm so ready." And she was, because

she wanted to be Travis's mistletoe kiss every Christmas, and she absolutely couldn't wait to be his bride.

"Love you." He touched his nose to hers, and Millie kissed him.

"Love you too."

Keep reading for Travis and Millie's wedding, as told by Travis's brother, Rex! Then go read **A COWBOY AND HIS DAUGHTER.**

If you want to rewind and go back to the beginning of December, there's another delicious cowboy billionaire Christmas romance for you in **A COWBOY AND HIS CHRISTMAS CRUSH**, where you'll get to see what happens with Russ and Janelle!

CHAPTER ONE OF A COWBOY AND HIS CHRISTMAS CRUSH

Russ Johnson stood outside, the faint music from the wedding dance behind him. He couldn't go back inside, not with his chest as deflated as it was. He was thrilled for Seth and Jenna, who'd been friends for a very long time. And he owed his last two months of dating the beautiful Janelle Stokes to Seth, who'd encouraged him to get out there and meet someone.

And he had. He and Janelle may not have seen each other every day for the past two months. Some people would call their relationship slow.

Russ didn't mind either of those things. When something awesome happened, he wanted to tell Janelle. When she had something to celebrate, he wanted to be the one who showed up with a cake.

And he'd thought they'd been getting along really well since the speed dating event in October. Slow and steady wins the race, he'd told himself.

Except he was losing. Big time.

Janelle had called him on Tuesday, and Russ had known from the moment she said his name that he wouldn't like what she was about to say.

And he hadn't. Because she'd broken up with him, citing her daughters as the reason why. He'd wanted to meet them. She'd freaked out.

It's fine, he'd texted her after she'd told him she didn't want to see him anymore. *I don't have to meet them until you're ready.*

He hadn't heard from her since.

He took a big breath and looked up into the starry sky. Behind him, the music stopped, and the door opened. People began piling outside, and Russ wanted to disappear again. But he joined the crowd instead, stepping over to Griffin and Rex while he scanned the crowd for Travis. He didn't see his brother, and Rex stepped out to help their parents get out of the fray.

The photographer came out and raised both of his hands. "Okay, everyone," he yelled. "Sparklers for everyone. Don't light them until I say, and you're going to hold them up like this." He held the sparkler right up above his head. "And wave them in short bursts. We only get one shot at this."

He started passing out sparklers, as did his assistant. Russ had no way to light the sparklers, but the photographer and his assistant started handing out matches too. He backed up to the doors and opened them a couple of inches. "Are the bride and groom ready?"

He must've gotten the go-ahead, because he turned back to the crowd outside. "All right, light 'em up."

The buzzing and fizzing of sparklers started, and the photographer called for Seth to bring Jenna outside. He did, and Russ could feel his brother's joy all the way at the back of the crowd. A cheer went up, and everyone lifted their sparklers and started waving them as taught.

The camera went *click, click, click* as the photographer walked backward, capturing the sparkler sendoff. He turned and took several pictures of the car, which Rex and Griffin had decorated. The décor was barely appropriate, but Seth and Jenna laughed at the cookies stuck to their car and ducked inside.

With them gone, the event concluded, and the vibrant

atmosphere fizzled along with the sparklers. Russ watched his burn all the way down, and then he put it in the pile with all the other burnt-out fireworks. He and his brothers still had an hour of clean-up to do, and he still didn't know where Travis had gotten to. *Probably with Millie*, Russ told himself, as he'd told his brother to go ask her to dance.

Russ found him inside, alone, folding up chairs. "You didn't come out for the sparkler thing?"

Travis shook his head, looking a bit dazed. Russ didn't have time to wonder what that was about, because they had to be out of the posh castle where Seth and Jenna had gotten married in exactly one hour.

He started helping with the chairs too, while others pulled down decorations, picked up centerpieces, and loaded everything into boxes to be taken outside. When everything was finally done, he got in the truck with Travis and started back to Chestnut Ranch.

Neither of them spoke, and Russ was grateful Travis wasn't the kind of brother who needed to know every detail of everything the moment it happened. He alone knew that Janelle had broken up with Russ—well, until that disastrous dinner conversation. Now everyone knew, and Russ was actually surprised his mother hadn't cornered him during the dancing to find out what had happened and then offered advice for how to fix it.

His momma meant well, he knew that. But she didn't understand that Janelle was as stubborn as the day was long.

She was smart too, and beautiful, with a wit that spoke right to Russ's sense of humor. She outclassed him in every way, and he told himself he should be grateful he got two months with her. But he couldn't help wanting more time. Wanting forever.

"How was the dance with Millie?" he asked when he went through the gate and onto the ranch.

"Good," Travis said.

"You gonna call her?"

His brother sighed and looked over at Russ. "Yeah. How do I do that?"

Russ grinned at Travis, who was a couple of years younger than him. "You just put in the numbers, and when she answers, you ask her to dinner. Easy."

"Easy," Travis said, scoffing afterward. He got out of the truck when Russ parked, but Russ stayed in the cab for another moment. Could he just tap a few times to pull up Janelle's contact info, call, and ask her to dinner?

"Yeah," he said to himself darkly. "If you want another slash on your heart." And he didn't. It was already hanging in shreds as it was, and Russ rather needed it to keep breathing.

RUSS SURVIVED SATURDAY AND SUNDAY, BECAUSE TRAVIS WAS there. They did minimal chores on the ranch on the weekends, and he and his brother could get the animals fed and watered in a couple of hours. He'd napped, and he'd stared at his phone, almost willing it to ring and have Janelle on the other end of the line.

Monday morning, Travis loaded up with the ranch hands that lived in the cabins along the entrance road, and they left to go move the cattle closer to the epicenter of the ranch.

Russ was glad he hadn't drawn that chore this time, but his loneliness reached a new high in a matter of hours. Griffin and Rex worked somewhere on the ranch, but Russ wasn't as close with them as he was Seth and Travis. He certainly didn't want to talk about Janelle with Rex, who thought it was fun to go out with one woman on Friday night and a different one for Saturday's lunch.

Evening found Russ standing on the back edge of the lawn, looking out over the wilder pastures of the ranch. In the distance, dogs barked and barked and barked. Russ normally loved dogs, but the increase of them on the ranch over the course of the last month had been too much.

And with Seth gone for the next couple of weeks, and Russ didn't even find the puppies cute anymore. Winner barked, as if she was the mother hen and was telling the other dogs to settle down. They didn't, and she ran along the grass line, barking every few feet.

"Enough," Russ told her. Eventually, he turned back to the house. He ate dinner, showered, slept. Then the next morning, he got up and did everything all over again. Travis returned that afternoon, and Rex ran to town for pizza and their mother's homemade root beer.

"To a successful relocation," Rex said, his voice so loud that it echoed through the kitchen.

Travis just grinned at him and took a bite of his supreme pizza. Russ was just glad there were more people in the homestead that night. It was a giant house, and he didn't like being in it alone.

"I'm goin' to shower," Travis said, and Russ picked up another piece of pizza. Griffin started telling a story about something Darren had said, and Russ was content to listen and laugh. A few minutes later, Travis came thundering down the stairs, his cowboy boots loud on the wood.

Rex was practically standing in the doorway already, and he ducked out to see what Travis was doing. He whistled and said, "Hoo boy, where are you off to?"

Russ exchanged a glance with Griffin, and said, "He's so loud."

"Try living with him," Griffin muttered, and they both moved into the living room, where Travis was putting one of his nicest dress hats on. He turned toward everyone and said, "I'm goin' out with Millie."

A smile crossed Russ's face. So he'd called her.

"Good for you, bro," Rex said.

"You look like you're going to throw up," Griffin said.

"Go," Russ said, stepping in front of the younger brothers. "Don't listen to them. Have fun." He smiled at Travis and nodded, because his brother needed to go out, and he needed the encouragement.

"What if—?"

"Nope," Russ said. "Now where are your keys?"

Travis patted his pockets, panic filling his face. "Shoot. I must've left them upstairs." He bolted back that way, and Russ shook his head.

"Don't give him grief over this," he said to the other two brothers. Rex held up both hands as if surrendering, and Griffin wandered back into the kitchen. Travis came back downstairs, his keys in his hand, and Russ said, "Have fun."

Travis said nothing as he left, and Russ chuckled and turned around. "I hope he calms down and has fun."

"He will," Rex said. "Travis gets along great with Millie. They'll be fine."

Russ nodded, wishing he was the one going out tonight. He didn't realize Rex had left until he brought him a piece of pizza from the kitchen. How much time did he lose thinking about Janelle?

"What about you and Janelle?" Rex asked, lifting his new piece of pizza to his lips. His eyes were sparkling, like he wanted all the dirt on the painful break-up. His half-smile said he'd definitely tease Russ, who wasn't in the mood.

"There's nothing about me and Janelle," Russ said.

"You like her though, right?"

"Of course I like her," Russ said, his voice growing as loud as Rex's. "I like her a whole lot. But what am I supposed to do? Drive over to her house and beg her to go out with me? She won't talk to me, Rex. She doesn't want me in her life. So liking her is irrelevant, isn't it?"

Rex lowered the pizza and stared. "I'm sorry, bro," he said, really quiet.

All the fight left Russ, and his shoulders slumped as the air whooshed out of his lungs. "Me too. Sorry, none of that was fair."

"I get it," Rex said. "No explanation needed." He fell back a step. "But if you like her as much as you say you do, she probably likes you too."

"Knock, knock?" a woman said, and Russ spun back toward the front door. It started to open, which meant it hadn't been latched all the way.

How much had Janelle heard?

Humiliation filled Russ, and he turned back to Rex, but he was gone. At least his brother had done one thing right that night. He'd brought dinner too, so Russ would give him two points.

"Janelle," he said, her name scratching in his throat. "What are you doing here?"

CHAPTER TWO OF A COWBOY AND HIS CHRISTMAS CRUSH

Janelle couldn't believe she had the courage to be standing on Russ's front porch. She also couldn't believe she'd heard his entire conversation with his brother.

"Janelle?" Russ said again, and she blinked.

"Yeah—yes," she said, clearing her throat. Her heart had been pounding for a solid hour, and she just wanted to calm down.

He came closer, and it was so unfair that he was so tall, with such broad shoulders, and that caring glint in his dark eyes. Janelle had always loved his eyes, from the very first moment she'd sat down across from him at the speed dating event during Chestnut Springs's Octoberfest.

"You have another dog with you," he said, looking down at the mutt panting at her feet.

"Yeah, uh..." She'd maybe used the dog to get herself out to the ranch. Somehow, she could deal with cheating husbands and angry wives as they became exes. She could argue for the rights of one of those parents in court until she got what she wanted. She owned and ran the biggest family law practice in the country.

And Russ Johnson made her heart flutter and her nerves fray.

He could also make her laugh faster than anyone else, and the man kissed her like she was worth something, and Janelle had been miserable for almost a week now.

"Look," she said, brushing her loose hair out of her eyes. "Someone brought the dog over, and they brought him to me, because they thought we were together."

Russ started nodding, the pain etched right on his face. He ducked his head, that dark gray cowboy hat hiding his eyes. She hadn't meant to hurt him, and she wanted to tell him she was miserable too. "And I brought him over here, because I want us to be together."

I like her a whole lot.

Janelle knew Russ liked her. When she'd called him to say she wanted to take a break, he'd gone silent. He accepted what she said, and she liked that he didn't argue back. Her ex would've argued back. In fact, she'd taken Henry back three times because of his excellent argumentative skills.

She should've never married another lawyer.

"You want us to be together," Russ said, lifting his eyes to hers. "You know what you're saying, right?"

"Yes," Janelle said. "And I told you last week, I just wanted a break. It wasn't a full break-*up*."

"No, what you said was that you didn't want me to meet your daughters." He held up one hand. "Which I'm fine with, sweetheart. Honest."

"It's not fair for you to call me sweetheart," she said, teasing him now. And he knew it.

"It's just me," he said, saying what he'd always said. "And when you meet my momma—"

"I know, I know," Janelle said, smiling. "She'll call me baby and sugar and sweetheart too."

Russ bent down and picked up the leash Janelle had put around the dog's neck. "I'll take him out to the enclosure, but I don't know where we're going to put him. We've got at least eight more dogs than we can house."

Janelle saw another opportunity zooming toward her, and she snatched at it. "I could take some," she said.

Russ's eyebrows went up, and she desperately wanted to swipe that cowboy hat from his head and kiss him. She licked her lips instead, her fantasies going down a path she couldn't follow. At least right now.

"You could take some?" Russ repeated. "Where are you going to put them?" He leaned in the doorway, easily the sexiest man alive in that moment.

"I have an old stable in my backyard," she said. "Maybe you could come help me fix it up, and I could probably put six or seven dogs back there."

Russ considered her, the corners of his mouth twitching up.

"What?" she asked, smiling at him.

"Do you know what to feed a dog?" he asked. "Or how often they need to go out? Or any of that?"

"No," she said. "That's why my awesome, handsome cowboy boyfriend will come help me…and the girls."

Russ's eyebrows went all the way up, and he folded his arms. She loved that he stayed silent during key moments, because the mystery of what he was thinking was hot.

"I get to meet the girls?" he asked.

"That's what you want, isn't it?" Janelle wanted that too. She was just overprotective of Kelly and Kadence.

"No, Janelle," he said, oh so soft and oh so sexy. "I don't know what you did or didn't hear. But I'm pretty sure it's obvious that what I want…is you."

The air left Janelle's lungs, because Russ Johnson always knew what to say and how to say it. Her fingers twitched toward his cowboy hat, and Russ chuckled.

"I saw that." His eyes twinkled like stars, and he took off his own cowboy hat this time. Janelle slipped one hand along the waistband of his jeans, his body heat so welcome. He enveloped her in an embrace, pressing his cowboy hat to her back.

"Russ," she whispered. "I like you a whole lot too."

"So you heard everything."

"I need to go slow," she said, closing her eyes and tipping her head back, an open invitation for him to kiss her.

"I know that, baby," he said, sliding his fingers around the back of her neck and into her hair. His lips touched hers in the next moment, and kissing Russ was like coming home. He took his time like he'd really missed her, and Janelle knew that he had. She hoped he could feel that she'd missed him too, and that she was sorry she'd freaked out about him meeting her kids.

THE FOLLOWING AFTERNOON, SHE PICKED THE GIRLS UP FROM school and said, "Okay, we have a new project."

"Another one?" Kelly asked, adjusting her backpack between her feet. "Mama, we're still making the brownies tonight, right?"

"Yes, yes," Janelle said, smiling at her oldest. "Chocolate and caramel swirl."

Kelly smiled. "So what's the new project?"

"It has to do with that dog someone brought over last night." Janelle made the left turn out of the school pick-up lane.

"You took it over to the ranch," Kelly said. "And then brought it back."

"They don't have room over there, and I told Russ we could put a few dogs in our stable. So we need to get it cleaned up for them." Janelle knew seven was more than "a few," but she didn't want to think too long about it. Otherwise, she'd wonder how she was going to keep them all happy and fed.

But it couldn't be that hard. The girls could help her put out fresh food and water morning and night. She had a fenced back-yard they could romp around in while she went to work and the girls went to school. And then she wouldn't have a canine sleeping in her bed, like she'd had last night.

She turned onto their street while the latest and greatest song came on. "Mama, turn it up," Kadence said from the back seat. Janelle smiled as she did, so glad she'd been pulling her hours back at the firm so that she could be there to pick up her girls in the afternoons.

She'd had a nanny for the past three years—since Henry had moved out—but she didn't want Mallory to be the one who knew her daughters. She didn't need to work as much as she did, and she wanted to be as good of a mother as everyone believed she was as a lawyer.

So she put up with the tween pop song her daughters knew every word to. Even Janelle could sing along, because the song was completely overplayed. She pulled into the garage and waited for the song to finish before turning off the car and getting out.

"Everyone in," she said. "Wash your hands and change your clothes. We'll work for an hour in the stables, and then it's brownie-making time."

Kelly cheered, and Janelle smiled at her. She'd taken off a huge bite this holiday season, but her ten-year-old loved baking and cooking, and Janelle had said they could put a post up every Sunday, asking all the clients and followers of the Bird Family Law social media to suggest the things they should make that week. And they'd make at least three of them.

The fun had only been going for a week, and since there hadn't been school last Wednesday, Thursday, or Friday, they'd made five of the dozens and dozens of suggestions.

This week, they'd chosen caramel swirl brownies, carrot cake muffins, and mini cheesecakes. They'd already made the carrot cake muffins last night, and Janelle wouldn't be surprised if they made five additional desserts that week.

The employees at the firm enjoyed the leftovers, and now that Janelle had gotten Russ to forgive her, she'd have another reason to pay the sixteen-year-old next door ten dollars to sit with her sleeping kids while she ran out to the ranch after dark.

She felt giddy at the idea of seeing him again that night, and she told herself that a woman her age shouldn't be sneaking off to see her boyfriend. As if on cue, her phone chimed and it was Audrey from next door, asking if she was still coming over that night.

Yep, Janelle sent. Thank you so much.

She got a smiley face and a thumbs up in return, and she put the step-stool in front of the sink so Kadence could reach to wash her hands. "Kel, did you wash?"

"Yes," her daughter called as she ran down the hall, and Janelle had the suspicion that her daughter had not washed her hands. Janelle was a bit of a germaphobe, and she worked with a lot of people. Always in and out of her building, with their kids, and their babies, and her daughters went to school with a plethora of kids who could have anything.

Her rule to wash hands after school eased her mind, though it probably didn't do anything to actually eliminate the germs she could be exposed to.

"Snacks?" she asked.

"That white popcorn," Kadence said, soaping up really good.

Janelle pumped some soap into her hands too and shared the running water with her daughter. "White popcorn comin' up." She washed, dried, and got down the bag of white popcorn before Kelly came back down the hall. She now wore an old pair of plaid pajama pants and a T-shirt that had been bleached at some point. "What do you want for a snack?"

"Cheese quesadillas," Kelly said.

"That's a meal," Janelle said. "We'll eat dinner while the brownies bake." She didn't have time for cheese quesadillas either.

"Granola bar," Kelly said.

"Great," Janelle said, giving her daughter the side-eye. "Wash your hands and get the box down. Let's go change, Kade." She gave Kelly a *don't even try to lie to me again* look as she guided Kadence out of the kitchen. "Pick something that can get dirty, okay?"

Kadence skipped into her room, and Janelle went into hers to

change out of her pencil skirt and silky blouse. She kicked off
her shoes, missing the cute heels she used to wear. But she had
bunions now from all those adorable shoes she'd worn in her
twenties. She'd been wearing orthopedic flats for over a decade
now, and she actually really liked them.

Several minutes later, she and her daughters went outside,
where the dog that had been dropped off last night came over to
greet them. He jumped away when Kelly reached for him, and
Janelle said, "Go on back to the stable, girls." She herded them
out of the gate, because Russ had warned her that stray dogs
were unpredictable.

"What should we name the dog?" Kadence asked.

"Name him?" Janelle stepped through the gate too.

"Yeah, if we're gonna keep him, he should have a name."

"Oh." Janelle took her daughter's hand. "What do you want
to name him?"

Kadence thought while they walked back to the stable.
"King."

"King it is," Janelle said, smiling. She wished she could bottle
up seven-year-olds, because they seemed to have the magic of
the world inside them. Kadence skipped everywhere, and even
mundane things like dandelions intrigued her.

Janelle reached the stable and opened the door, the smell of
something old and dusty coming out. "Oh, boy," she said, looking
at the wreck that existed inside the stable. Her first thought was
to call Russ and invite him over. But that wouldn't be fair,
because he had a ton of work to do at his own ranch. With his
brother gone, Russ was working more than usual, and she'd
agreed to go consult with him about taking on half a dozen dogs
that night, after the girls were down for the night.

Janelle turned back to her kids. "Kelly, go grab the broom
from the garage. Kadence, see if you can get the garbage can we
use for weeds."

The girls turned to go do the things she wanted, and Janelle
reached for a pair of gloves on the shelf by the door. She could

do this for one hour, just to be able to tell Russ that she hadn't done nothing that day. She didn't want him to think she was using him, and though he'd kissed her last night and said they were good, Janelle knew he didn't trust her completely.

She also knew trust was built one brick at a time. One day at a time. One good experience at a time. So she'd put the girls to bed, drive out to the ranch, and hope she could have another amazing night with Russ Johnson.

Her phone blitzed out a high-pitched noise, and her heartbeat leapt over itself. She'd assigned that chime to Russ, and while she could hear Kadence pulling the garbage can across the cement, she hurried to pull out her phone.

I have something to show you tonight.

Great, she tapped out. *Can't wait.*

Oh, and how does hot chocolate sound?

"Amazing," she whispered, a smile crossing her face.

"What, Mama?" Kadence said, arriving behind her out of breath.

"Nothing." Janelle pocketed her phone and reached for the garbage can. "Nice job, Kade. Now, we're going to fill this thing up."

She'd work, and she'd bake with the girls, because there would be nothing better with hot chocolate than caramel swirl brownies.

Can Russ learn to trust Janelle, or will his Christmas crush stay that way? Find out in the **A COWBOY AND HIS CHRISTMAS CRUSH**.

CHAPTER ONE OF A COWBOY AND HIS DAUGHTER

R ex Johnson liked weddings, because there was always a lot of available women clamoring for the bouquet. They had their hair done up, their makeup perfect, and those high heels he liked a whole lot.

He sat in the front row with the rest of his family, his mother already weeping and Travis hadn't even come out to the altar yet. As the baby brother, Rex had a special relationship with his momma, and he reached over and took her hand in his.

She squeezed his hand, and he knew she wanted this marital bliss for all of her sons, including him. He didn't want to disappoint her, but he wasn't going to get married. That was why he kept the women he dated at arm's length, why he only went out with them for a maximum of two months, whether he liked them or not. And most of the time, he knew after the first or second date if a woman would even get that long on his arm.

His brothers thought he was a player. Even Griffin, the next oldest brother and the one Rex lived with full time in town, thought Rex was a bit cruel to women. What they didn't know was that Rex had given his heart away five years ago. He couldn't give away what he didn't have, but he didn't want to stay home every weekend either.

Most of the women he went out with knew what they were getting, and those that didn't, Rex told them the rules.

Yes, he had rules, and he wasn't sorry about them.

The twittering in the crowd increased, and Rex looked to his right to see Travis had come outside. Finally. The sooner this wedding got started, the sooner it would end. His brother took his spot at the altar, shook hands with the preacher, and nodded as the other man said something.

Rex hadn't gotten the fancy ranch wedding, with miles of flowers and lace and the rich, black tuxedo with the matching cowboy hat. He hadn't had people rushing around to make sure all the chairs were perfectly aligned or that the guest book sat at a perfect forty-five-degree angle from the five-tier cake.

He'd dressed in the nicest clothes he had and met the woman of his dreams at City Hall in downtown Bourne. Her sister and her husband had been there as witnesses, and Rex had smiled through the whole thing.

He'd smiled when Holly told him she was pregnant. Smiled at her parents when they'd gone to tell them. Smiled, smiled, smiled.

Rex was tired of smiling.

He hadn't been smiling when Holly had lost their baby. Or when she'd said she'd made a mistake and then filed for divorce only two months after they'd said I-do. Or when she'd left for work one morning and never came home.

He'd packed up everything they'd owned and put it in storage, where it still remained in a facility on the outskirts of Chestnut Springs. He wasn't sure why he'd chosen to store it so close, as he hadn't heard from Holly in the five years since all of that had happened, and he wasn't living in his hometown at the time.

Maybe for distance. In the end, he'd returned to Chestnut Springs a few years later, and he'd been living with Griffin in the downtown home they'd gone in on together for three years now.

The music started, and a hush fell over the crowd as they

stood. Rex did too, going through all the motions. He was
happy for Travis and Millie. He was. They made the perfect
couple, and Travis had always been a bit quiet when it came to
women.

Rex, on the other hand, was the complete opposite. He
smiled at Millie as she came down the aisle with his father. Hers
apparently lived somewhere else, and they didn't have a great
relationship.

Every step his father took over the white river rock was slow
and looked painful. Rex really didn't know how he was going to
leave in a few short months to work a service mission in the
Dominican Republic, but Mom insisted they were going, that
the doctors said it was okay.

Daddy kissed Millie's cheek and passed her to Travis, who
hugged him. Rex's heart—the little he had left—swelled, and he
felt a brief flash of the perfect family love he shared with his
parents and brothers.

He did love them, and he enjoyed the Thursday night dinners
at his parents' house and the Sunday afternoon meals and activities that still took place at the ranch. Seth and Jenna came every
week, and with Travis and Millie living in the front corner of the
ranch, Rex assumed they'd keep coming too.

"Sit down," Griffin hissed, pulling on Rex's sleeve. He practically fell backward into his seat, and his face heated.

"Pay attention, baby," his mom whispered to him, and Rex
tried to focus on what was happening in front of him. The pastor
spoke about nice things, about keeping the lines of communica-
tion open, of working through problems instead of letting them
fester into bigger things.

Millie and Travis each read vows while the gentle spring
breeze blew under the tent, and then the pastor pronounced
them husband and wife. Travis grinned at his new wife, dipped
her though she squealed, and kissed her.

Rex cheered and clapped the loudest, as always. He knew he
had a loud voice, and he didn't even try to quiet it. The new

bride and groom went down the aisle to the applause, and everyone stood up.

It seemed like a whole lot of work for a ten-minute ceremony. At least to Rex, and he once again found himself thinking about the simplicity of his marriage. He'd known it wasn't what Holly wanted, but with the time and money constraints they'd had, it was all Rex could give her.

Now that his bank account was considerably bigger, he wondered what kind of wedding they'd have now.

You've got to stop, he told himself sternly. Most days, he did just fine not thinking about Holly and the baby that wasn't meant to be. He'd kept the secret from everyone he knew for five long years, and if he didn't think about it, the burden was easier to carry.

But weddings—especially his brother's—had really brought back the memories in full force. He followed his parents down the path toward the butterfly gardens at Serendipity, thinking he'd probably like an outdoor wedding now too.

That so wasn't banishing the thoughts of marriage and weddings and Holly from his mind, but Rex couldn't help it. He stayed quiet, his cowboy boots making the most noise as they walked through the gardens and out to the parking lot.

Jenna had a sprawling patio that was heated and cooled, and the wedding dinner would take place over there. After that, Millie and Travis had decided to forgo any type of formal dance, and instead, they'd rented a couple of hot air balloons for guests to enjoy as they celebrated with an ice cream bar for anyone who hadn't been invited to the family dinner.

Rex hadn't had a reception either, and his frustration with himself grew.

"See you over there," his mother said, and Rex looked up from the ground to find Griffin helping her behind the wheel of the minivan she drove now. Daddy couldn't drive with his leg, and most of the time, Rex thought his mother shouldn't be driving either.

"Ready?" Griffin asked as he closed the door behind their mother.

Rex handed him the keys in response. "You drive."

"What's goin' on with you?" he asked. "You've been real quiet during all of this."

Rex shrugged, because he didn't want to say what was going on with him. Maybe he should just try calling Holly again. He'd done that for the first few months after she'd left, and she hadn't answered once. He hadn't known if her number was the same, and he was certain it wasn't now.

He didn't know if she was still in the state, though he suspected she was. She'd been born and raised in the Texas Hill Country, and she'd told him once during their year-long relationship that she couldn't imagine living anywhere else.

"Not even Dallas or San Antonio?" he'd asked.

"Definitely not," she said. "I'm a country girl, Rex."

He'd laughed, because he was a country boy too, and he sure had loved Holly Rasmussen. With effort, he pushed her out of his mind and focused on the radio station Griffin had set.

He liked country music as much as the next red-blooded cowboy, but Rex's tastes were more on the modern side than Griffin's. He didn't reach over to change the station, though, something he'd done in the past. He and his brother could argue the whole way to the ranch about what to listen to.

"I'm going to apply for that camp counselorship again," Griffin said, and Rex looked over at his brother.

"Is it that time already?"

"Yeah," he said. "Applications are due by April fifteenth. Do you want to do it with me?"

"Maybe," Rex said. He and Griffin had both gone to Camp Clear Creek out near Lake Marble Falls and Horseshoe Bay in the Hill Country. It was beautiful country, and Rex liked being outside. He'd had a group of six boys every two weeks for three months, and he loved boating, hiking, fishing, and hunting.

"Just fill out an application with me," Griffin said. "You can change your mind later."

"You don't need to fill out an application," Rex said. "You can just email Toni." He swung his gaze to his brother and found Griffin's face turning bright red. He burst out laughing, connecting all the dots in an instant.

"What?" Griffin asked, obviously not amused.

"You still have a thing for Toni."

"I do not," Griffin said. "First of all, the word *still* is all wrong. It implies I had a thing before and now I *still* do, which is totally not true."

"Mm hm," Rex said, because he knew Griffin better than anyone. And whether or not Griffin admitted that he'd had a cowboy crush on their boss last summer didn't mean he didn't. Because he totally did. "Well, I'm sure she's always looking for good counselors."

"So maybe you shouldn't apply," Griffin quipped, and Rex laughed again. "Besides, I heard she left Clear Creek, which is why I do need to apply."

"All right," Rex said. "Apply then."

"You don't want to?"

Rex watched the last of the town go by before Griffin started down the curvy road that led to the ranch. "You know what? I'm going to stick closer to home this summer. I'll handle all of your chores at the ranch."

Griffin snorted. "Right. You'll hire someone the moment you can. You can't even get out of bed before nine-thirty."

"I can," Rex said. "I just don't like to."

"You're not even a real cowboy," Griffin said with a chuckle.

"Getting up at the crack of dawn isn't a characteristic of a cowboy," Rex said, reaching up and settling his hat on his head. He had all the proper attire to make him a cowboy, and that was good enough for him.

Griffin eased up on the gas pedal, and Rex looked over at him. "What?"

"I don't know where my phone is."

"Are you kidding me right now?" Rex started lifting up the sunglasses cases in the console between them. "It's not here."

Griffin was notorious for losing his phone. Leaving it places. Not knowing where it was. Another round of annoyance pulled through Rex, especially when Griffin slowed and pulled over. "I know where it is. I left it in the groom's dressing room. On the windowsill."

"Do you need it right now?" he asked

"Yes," Griffin said, no room for negotiation.

"We're going to be late," Rex said.

"Text Seth with your phone," he said. "It'll be fine."

"Fine." Rex scoffed and pulled out his phone and texted their oldest brother. He was so changing the radio station while Griffin ran back inside the fancy building at Serendipity Seeds to get his device.

Several minutes later, Griffin pulled up to the curb and dashed off without even closing the driver's side door. Rex promptly leaned over and changed the radio station to something that played more of the country rock he liked and sighed as he settled back into his seat, reaching to put his window down so the breeze would blow through the cab of the truck.

"Come on, baby doll." The woman's voice stirred something in Rex, and he turned to look out his window.

A little girl had crouched down on the path, her dark hair curly and wispy as she examined something on the ground.

Rex couldn't see her mother, but he heard her say, "Sarah, come on. We're going to be late."

That voice.

Rex got out of the truck and looked further down the path to find a dark-haired woman standing there, wearing a pair of jeans and a T-shirt with a lightning bolt on the front.

"Holly?" he asked, his voice barely meeting his own ears. But it couldn't be Holly. Not his Holly.

She sure did look like her, though, and Rex took another step toward the little girl. "Hey," he said, making his voice as gentle as he could. The girl, who'd ignored her mother completely, looked up at him. She was beautiful, with deep, dark eyes and the same olive skin Holly had possessed. She couldn't be older than four or five, as her face still carried some of the roundness that chubby babies had.

"What're you lookin' at?" He crouched next to her, the sound of the gravel crunching as the woman came closer.

"Sarah," she said, her voice almost a bark.

Rex straightened, and now that Holly was closer, he totally knew it was her. Number one, his wounded heart was thrashing inside his chest, screaming about how this woman held the missing bits of it.

"Holly," he said, and it wasn't a question this time.

Pure panic crossed her face, and she fell back a step, one hand coming up to cover her mouth. He still heard her when she said, "Rex."

He looked back and forth between her and the little girl, beyond desperate to know what in the world was going on. But for maybe the first time in his life, he stayed quiet, giving his ex-wife the opportunity to explain.

CHAPTER TWO OF A COWBOY AND HIS DAUGHTER

Holly Rasmussen stared at the tall, dark, deliciously handsome cowboy in front of her. Rex Johnson, the man who'd been haunting her for five long years. The man she saw every time she looked into her daughter's eyes. The man she'd hoped to never see again.

"Well?" he prompted, and Holly blinked her way out of the trance she'd fallen into.

"How are you?" she asked, but he shook his head.

"Try again."

She reached for Sarah's hand, the tears coming more easily than her daughter did. Thankfully, the little girl slipped her dirty hand into Holly's, and she glanced down at her. She'd just turned five, and if Holly's memory was right, Rex was very good at math.

And her memory was right.

"Baby doll," she said, her voice tight, scared. She hated that seeing him made her feel this way. He'd once made her feel loved and cherished, like nothing in the world could go wrong.

She'd showed him, though. With her, disaster always struck.

"This is Rex Johnson," she said, and the little girl looked up at her father. "Rex." She cleared her throat, cursing herself for agreeing to come to Chestnut Springs. She knew Rex was from this town, but she'd reasoned that she'd be here for less than a day, and surely she wouldn't run into him.

"Holly," her mother called, and Holly pressed her eyes closed. Wow, she didn't want her mom to see Rex. Everything started crashing around her, every half-truth she'd told. Every lie. Every secret. Every day for the past five years.

She turned around and said, "Go tell Gramma I need a minute," to Sarah. She gave her a quick kiss, glad when the little girl did what she'd asked.

"Gramma," Rex said. "She's your daughter." He took a step closer to her, those dark-as-midnight eyes sparking and catching hers. "Is she *my* daughter?"

Holly couldn't lie about this. She also couldn't vocalize it, so she just nodded.

Rex searched her face, more and more anger entering his expression than Holly liked. She'd expected it, of course. Or had she? She'd never imagined seeing Rex again, and she honestly didn't know what to expect next.

"You didn't lose the baby?" he asked, his voice hoarse and cut to shreds.

"No," she whispered.

He stepped back and blew out his breath. "You just didn't tell me. You disappeared in the middle of the night. You hated me that much?" He shook his head, his fists clenching and unclenching. "You know what? I don't care." He leaned closer and closer, his fury a scent in the air. "You're a terrible, terrible person. I can't believe I've wasted six years of my life thinking about you."

Footsteps sounded behind her, but she couldn't move. *You're a terrible, terrible person,* rang through her entire soul.

He wasn't wrong.

She just hadn't expected to hear him say such things. Her mother certainly had. Her grandmother. Everyone. But Holly couldn't explain herself to them, because she didn't understand why she'd done certain things either.

"Ready?" a man asked, and he joined Rex's side. He definitely belonged to Rex, and Holly guessed he was one of his four brothers. She'd never met any of them, and Rex had basically given up everything to be with her.

"Who's this?" he asked, and Rex shook his head, his jaw clenched.

"No one. Let's go." He turned away from her, and Holly flinched. Wow, that hurt. *No one.*

You started it, she thought, and she felt like she'd gone backward five years in only five minutes.

The two cowboys walked away from her, Rex's brother casting a worried look over his shoulder as he went. Rex got in the truck, almost immediately opening the door and coming back toward her.

"Is she really mine?" he asked in a loud voice from several paces away.

"Yes," Hollly said.

"Then I want to see her," he said. "What's your number?"

"I'm only in town for a wedding today," she said.

He laughed, the sound high and cruel. "Get a hotel, then, Holly. Because if she's my kid, I'm suing you for custody."

"There's no if, Rex," she said, finally finding her voice. "You're the only man I've ever been with."

"Not comforting," he said, holding his phone out. "I'm serious. Give me your number."

Holly looked helplessly at the other brother, who'd come closer too. "What's going on?"

"She's my ex-wife," Rex practically bellowed. "And she told me she'd lost our baby. But I just met her." He glared at her. "I want your number, and if you leave town, I'm filing kidnapping charges."

Tears streamed down Holly's face, but she nodded. She recited her number, and Rex tapped it into his phone. Her device in her back pocket buzzed, and he said, "I just texted you.

Text me where you're staying, and I'll come pick her up in the morning."

"What are you going to do?" she asked.

"My brother got married today," Rex said. "So I'm going to keep everything real quiet for right now. And then I'm going to make sure I get to see my daughter whenever I want." He took one menacing step toward her. "You stole five years from me. I gave you *everything*." He broke then, and Holly's heart wailed and wailed.

She watched him cover his emotions with that furious mask again, and he said, "If you don't text me, I'll call the police."

"I'll text you," she said, wondering how she was going to explain having to stay in town to her mother.

He turned back to his brother, who wore a look of complete shock on his face. So Rex had kept their secret this whole time. Rex marched past the brother and got in the fancy pickup truck parked at the curb. The brother stared at her, so many questions in his eyes.

Then he turned and got behind the wheel, driving away in the next moment.

Holly watched the truck go, and then she collapsed onto the nearest bench and sobbed.

"I don't know, Momma," she said later that night, after the wedding. "But I'm staying for a bit. I have a place for me and Sarah." She glanced around at the tiny studio room she'd gotten for the next week.

"Who's going to take care of Sarah?" Momma asked. "You're really going to get a job up there? Why?"

Holly drew in a deep breath. "I ran into Rex today."

For maybe the first time in her life, Momma had nothing to say. When Holly had taken Rex to meet her parents and tell them she was pregnant, her mother had had plenty to say. A born-and-raised Texan, she didn't hold back her opinions.

"He knows about Sarah," Holly continued.

"Dear Lord in Heaven," her mother said, her voice breathless.

"I'm ready, Momma," she said. "I've been telling you that for months."

"I know," Momma said. "But I thought you'd start easy. Get a job, and I'd take care of Sarah during the day."

"Well, I'm going to get a job up here," she said. "They have daycares and stuff here."

"You can't afford that," her mother said. "Where are you even staying? You can't afford anything in Chestnut Springs."

Holly pressed her eyes closed against the questions. Her momma had fired them at her like this when she'd shown up five years ago, divorced and six months pregnant. She'd been living with her parents ever since, fading in and out of depressive episodes that didn't leave her much time to learn how to be a mother.

But she'd been doing really well for a long time now. Over a year. Once her father had passed away and Holly had seen her mother start to slide, she'd pulled herself together and gotten help. She still talked to a therapist every day through an app, with weekly video appointments.

And she was ready to be the mother Sarah needed. Her mother had been resistant, because she loved playing the hero. And if Holly got back on her own feet and started taking care of herself and her daughter, Momma couldn't give herself a medal at the end of every day.

"Momma," she said, when she realized her mother was still talking. "I'm thirty-one years old."

You're a terrible, terrible person.

"I can do this," she said. "It's time to come clean. Tell the truth. Move on."

"In Chestnut Springs?"

"I owe Rex a proper apology and explanation," she said quietly, powerful guilt moving through her. "Aren't you the one who always says that?"

"Yes, but—"

"Momma," she said over her mother, and it felt good to stand up to Momma. "I'll call you tomorrow, okay?"

A long silence came through the line, and Holly knew her mother was working through a lot of her own issues. "Okay," she finally said, and Holly nodded. She hung up and looked over to the sleeping form of Sarah.

A pretty little girl, Sarah had brought more joy and light into Holly's life than anything else.

"Except Rex," she murmured, because that man had been her whole world.

You're a terrible, terrible person.

She knew an apology wouldn't go far with Rex. The man loved deeply, and she heard his angry voice as he accused her of stealing six years of his life. As he threatened to call the police. She reached over and stroked Sarah's hair, the soft, silky quality of it helping her feel a tiny pinprick of hope.

"You're better now," she whispered to herself. "Maybe you can fix things with Rex, too."

She'd texted him the name of the motel she'd found, and he said he'd be there at nine o'clock in the morning. Holly hadn't brought clothes to Chestnut Springs, because she'd planned to stay for just one day.

Momma was right; she didn't have much money. But she had a credit card, and she could get a few things for the week she'd be here.

"Might be longer," she said to herself, because she remembered Rex being the kind of man that fought for what he wanted. He'd called her for six straight months after she'd vanished from his life. He'd gone to her parents' house. He'd called her friends. Gone to talk to her boss.

And when he found out where she'd been, maybe he'd understand.

Maybe.

Hopefully.

"Please," she prayed, because she was ready to move forward, and she couldn't if Rex didn't come with her.

Oh, dear, I sure hope Rex and Holly can figure things out! Find out if they can in **A COWBOY AND HIS DAUGHTER**.

CHESTNUT RANCH ROMANCE

Book 1: A Cowboy and his Neighbor: Best friends and neighbors shouldn't share a kiss...

Book 2: A Cowboy and his Mistletoe Kiss: He wasn't supposed to kiss her. Can Travis and Millie find a way to turn their mistletoe kiss into true love?

Book 3: A Cowboy and his Christmas Crush: Can a Christmas crush and their mutual love of rescuing dogs bring them back together?

Book 4: A Cowboy and his Daughter: They were married for a few months. She lost their baby...or so he thought.

Book 5: A Cowboy and his Boss: She's his boss. He's had a crush on her for a couple of summers now. Can Toni and Griffin mix business and pleasure while making sure the teens they're in charge of stay in line?

Book 6: A Cowboy and his Fake Marriage: She needs a husband to keep her ranch...can she convince the cowboy next-door to marry her?

Book 7: A Cowboy and his Secret Kiss: He likes the pretty adventure guide next door, but she wants to keep their relationship off the grid. Can he kiss her in secret and keep his heart intact?

Book 8: A Cowboy and his Skipped Christmas: He's been in love with her forever. She's told him no more times than either of them can count. Can Theo and Sorrell find their way through past pain to a happy future together?

ABOUT EMMY

Emmy is a Midwest mom who loves dogs, cowboys, and Texas. She's been writing for years and loves weaving stories of love, hope, and second chances.

Printed in Great Britain
by Amazon

11957520R00140